GHOSTS IN THE GARDEN

GHOSTS IN THE GARDEN

JUDITH SILVERTHORNE

Edited by Anne Patton
Book designed by Jamie Olson
Typeset by Susan Buck
Edwardian Garden Map courtesy Government House
Chapter opening graphic by Stephanie Campbell
Printed and bound in Canada

Library and Archives Canada Cataloguing in Publication

Silverthorne, Judith, author
    Ghosts in the garden / Judith Silverthorne.

Issued in print and electronic formats.
ISBN 978-1-55050-905-2 (softcover).--ISBN 978-1-55050-906-9 (PDF).--
ISBN 978-1-55050-907-6 (EPUB).--ISBN 978-1-55050-908-3 (Kindle)

    I. Title.

PS8587.I2763G46 2017   jC813'.54   C2016-907251-7
                                                  C2016-907252-5

Library of Congress Control Number 2016957179

2517 Victoria Avenue
Regina, Saskatchewan
Canada S4P 0T2
www.coteaubooks.com

Available in Canada from:
Publishers Group Canada
2440 Viking Way
Richmond, British Columbia
Canada V6V 1N2

10 9 8 7 6 5 4 3 2

Available in the US from:
Orca Book Publishers
www.orcabook.com
1-800-210-5277

Coteau Books gratefully acknowledges the financial support of its publishing program by: the Saskatchewan Arts Board, The Canada Council for the Arts, the Government of Saskatchewan through Creative Saskatchewan, the City of Regina. We further acknowledge the [financial] support of the Government of Canada. Nous reconnaissons l'appui [financier] du gouvernement du Canada.

For Georgie and Caoimhe

For nearly five years, I have had the privilege of working in Government House. Every time I enter my offices in the north wing, or walk through the museum on my way to host an event in the Ballroom, I feel as though I am stepping back in time. Not only am I surrounded by the splendour of the restored Vice-Regal residence, our clever museum staff have added life-sized mannequins as well as sound effects tailored for each room, all of which combine to bring history to life.

I love how Judith Silverthorne explores the fascinating past of this historic property through the curious Sam and J.J., who get more than they bargained for when they take a peek behind a basement door.

Judith's well-researched story draws from the actual people and events of the House and I must admit, I learned about a few historic figures I had not heard of before! Of course, this isn't a history book, it's a very fun story, and has caused me to look over my shoulder a few times, especially when I'm working late at night.

I am grateful to Judith for sparking my imagination about this grand old building. I hope you enjoy *Ghosts of Government House* as much as I did, and I warmly welcome you to visit the real Government House to catch a glimpse of the past.

Her Honour the Honourable Vaughn Solomon Schofield
Lieutenant Governor of Saskatchewan

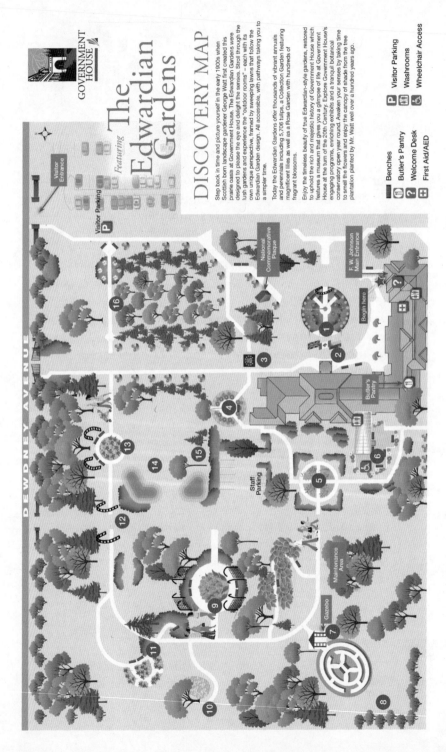

GOVERNMENT HOUSE

Featuring

The Edwardian Gardens

DISCOVERY MAP

Step back in time and picture yourself in the early 1900s when Scottish born landscape gardener George Watt first created this prairie oasis at Government House. The Edwardian Gardens were designed to please the eye and delight the senses. Stroll through the lush gardens and experience the "outdoor rooms" - each with its own unique perspective, framed by sweeping lawns that follow the Edwardian Garden design. All accessible, with pathways taking you to a simpler time.

Today the Edwardian Gardens offer thousands of vibrant annuals and perennials including 5,706 tulips, a Collection Garden featuring magnificent lilies as well as a Rose Garden with hundreds of fragrant blossoms.

Enjoy the timeless beauty of true Edwardian-style gardens, restored to uphold the rich and majestic history of Government House which features a museum that gives you a glimpse of life at Government House at the turn of the 20th Century. Explore Government House's engaging programs, enriching exhibits and a tranquil botanical conservatory open year round. Awaken your senses by taking time to smell the flowers and enjoy the canopy of shade from the tree plantation planted by Mr. Watt well over a hundred years ago.

Benches
Butler's Pantry
Welcome Desk
First Aid/AED

Visitor Parking
Washrooms
Wheelchair Access

DEWDNEY AVENUE

Visitor Entrance

Visitor Parking

National Commemorative Plaque

F. W. Johnson Main Entrance

Begin here

Butler's Pantry

Staff Parking

Maintenance Area

Gazebo

The Edwardian Gardens

George Watt's vision for an oasis on the prairies

In the early 1900s, the Edwardian Gardens of Government House stood out as an oasis against Regina's treeless landscape. Producing these British-style gardens in Saskatchewan's harsh climate was no small feat and would not have been achieved without the name of George Watt.

Watt's legacy can be seen not only in the grounds surrounding Government House, but throughout the landscape of Saskatchewan's capital city. The elm trees and caragana bushes that he planted were the first of their kind to be introduced in Regina and have since come to characterize the city's topography.

By donating both his time and trees, Watt also contributed to municipal projects, including the beautification of Victoria Park and Wascana Park. After leaving Government House in 1908, Watt went on to work for the Government of Saskatchewan and was involved in the development of the Legislative Building grounds.

George Watt in the conservatory c.1905

Points of Interest

1. Ceremonial Circle
As you begin to explore the majestic grounds surrounding Government House you are welcomed by the Ceremonial Circle, which was part of the original grounds design dating back to 1891. Taking a panoramic view of this historic building you will see the additions and transformation of Government House over the last hundred years. Facing west is the original structure built in 1891. To the south, is the ballroom added in 1928 and to the east of the ballroom, the Queen Elizabeth II Wing, which was opened by Her Majesty in 2005.

2. Portico
For many years, this grand portico, or porte-cochère, protected the occupants from bad weather and served as the main entrance for visitors from all over the world. Today this area is reserved for visiting dignitaries and special guests of the Lieutenant Governor.

3. Lynda Haverstock Ceremonial Drive
As you walk along Ceremonial Drive, you will notice the Lieutenant Governor's emblem is embedded in the driveway. This majestic entrance and driveway has always been exclusively reserved for the Lieutenant Governor and the Premier of Saskatchewan.

4. Lieutenant Governor's Meeting Place
As you reach the north end of Government House, you will find one of the Lieutenant Governor's favourite places to host guests. This unique circular "outdoor room" surrounds you with an impressive view of the Edwardian Gardens.

5. Herb Garden
For more than 100 years, this herb garden has served Government House's kitchen. Many of the tasty treats served at the Government House Historical Society Victorian Teas feature delectable herbs from this garden. In 2012, the Herb garden was visited by the Duke and Duchess of Cornwall as part of their visit to Government House during the Queen's Diamond Jubilee celebrations.

6. Conservatory
Continuing to the southwest side of the building, you will find the conservatory that was added on to Government House in 1901 and moved to this location in 1926. The conservatory has survived the test of time and weather, offering a botanical year-round retreat for visitors coming to Government House.

7. Hedge Maze
In the early 1900s, George Watt planted the first caragana bushes in Regina at Government House. They became very popular with farmers as shelterbelts and can now be found throughout the Prairie landscapes. To honour Watt's legacy, this hedge maze was planted with caragana bushes in 2010.

8. Consular Grove
Outlining the southwest corner of the gardens is the Consular Grove, where each of Saskatchewan's Honourary Consuls planted a tree in 2011 to represent their country. Each tree was given an identification tag indicating the Honourary Consul, country, as well as the species of tree.

9. Netherlands Liberation Garden
As you walk to the northeast, you come to the beautiful Netherlands Liberation Garden. In 1984, the Dutch Government sent a gift of 5,706 tulips as a tribute to each Canadian soldier buried in the Netherlands during WWII.

10. Servants' Foundation
West of the Netherlands Liberation Garden is a walkway that leads to the remains of a building foundation. It is likely that this foundation was a servants' house for the numerous staff members dedicated to the growth and operations of Government House.

11. Collection Garden
To the north is one of Government House's most vibrant, picturesque gardens; the Collection Garden features many stunning traditional and hybrid lilies showcasing an array of colour.

12. Service Road
On your way to the Rose Garden, you will cross the service road. This road has been used for service access since the house was completed in 1891. From carriage drivers to caterers, this driveway has facilitated the behind-the-scenes maintenance of Government House since its earliest days.

13. Rose Garden
Stop and smell the roses! Dwarf Dahlias border this fragrant flower bed featuring over 55 gorgeous rose bushes of varying types.

14. North Lawn
To the south of the Rose Garden is an area that was used for a variety of activities prior to 1945, including a children's playground in the summer and a skating rink in the winter. Today this open green space is used for summer picnics and entertainment during the Lieutenant Governor's Garden Party on July 1, which attracts over 2,000 visitors annually.

15. Governor General's Tree
The Governor General's Tree that was planted by Her Excellency Michaëlle Jean on her farewell tour of Canada in 2011 is found at the south end of the north lawn. It is a Burr Oak tree.

16. Tree Plantation
In 1907, Lieutenant Governor Forget, along with George Watt, travelled to Banff and brought back 4,600 spruce saplings to be planted at Government House. With the passage of time, a few original trees still remain today. In addition to the tree plantation, commemorative trees were planted by Canada's premiers in 2009 when they met at Government House for the annual Council of the Federation. Customized tree tags were created to identify each premier's province and its date of confederation.

CHAPTER ONE

J.J. AND HER FRIEND, Sam, ran down the hall in the basement of Government House. Their teacher had given them permission to get a drink at the water fountain.

After the girls each had a drink, J.J. stood with her hands on her hips, watching Sam continue down the wide hall.

"Hurry up, Sam. We're going to get in trouble again if we don't get right back."

A woman in a blue flowered dress passed J.J. with a smile. Momentarily distracted, J.J. watched the woman glide gracefully up the stairs that led back up to the main floor. She almost seemed to float.

J.J. turned her attention back to Sam, who was heading in the opposite direction from the activity room filled with their classmates. They were supposed to be returning to work on their posters, not exploring the premises.

"I just want to see what's down here. You don't have to come," Sam said, and disappeared around a corner.

J.J. groaned. Sam knew that her curiosity always won out.

THEIR GRADE FIVE class was on a school trip to learn more about the former residence of Lieutenant Governors in Saskatchewan. Some said the impressive mansion was haunted. From previous experience, J.J. knew this to be true.

"I hope we don't find any more ghosts right now," she said. Even though they had formed the J.J. and Sam Ghost Detective Agency, she didn't want to run into any ghosts when they were supposed to be with the other students. Besides, they didn't have any of their ghost-detecting gear with them.

"We'll just take a quick peek to see where this leads," said Sam. Once J.J. joined her, Sam opened a heavy metal door into a narrower, shorter hallway. The door wheezed shut behind them. Overhead, the fluorescent lights flickered.

"I don't like this." J.J. eyed Sam nervously. "Let's go back."

"We won't be long," Sam said, as the lights flickered again. "Just don't think about ghosts. Besides, the only ghost we're likely to see down here is the harmless old gardener, George Watt."

Suddenly, they were plunged into darkness.

J.J. gave a little gasp. Sam opened the door again to the main hallway. Lights still gleamed, showing the way they'd come.

"The power hasn't gone out everywhere, so why is there no light here?" J.J. asked. She shivered. She knew the lighting in Government House seemed to be faulty, and it usually meant something mysterious was going on in the house.

"Let's wait until our eyes adjust to find out." Sam let

the door wheeze shut once more. "I figure we're probably underneath the ballroom."

J.J. stalled. "I really don't like this at all. It's too dark down here." She moved close to Sam.

Their breathing was the only sound.

After a few moments, J.J. could see a faint glow of daylight coming from a small window at the end of the hall. Strangely, the hallway seemed much longer than it had been moments before.

"This is still too dark." J.J. clutched Sam's arm. She really, really didn't want to come across a ghost right now. Most of the ghosts they'd seen on previous visits had been in daylight.

"How about we come back another time with our flashlights and ghost detecting equipment?" She felt her pulse quicken, and she tried to pull Sam back the way they'd come.

Sam didn't budge.

"We'll come sometime when we're not with the class." J.J. grimaced at the thought of their classmates laughing at them.

Sam pulled J.J. forward. "We'll just take a quick look and be back before anything happens or anyone misses us."

"I don't want to trip and fall." J.J. already had bandages on her scraped knees from learning to skateboard.

"We'll be fine." Sam took J.J.'s icy hand and they inched their way down the almost dark hallway.

Sam swept her hand along the rough cement wall.

"There must be a light switch somewhere."

"Overhead, but don't grab *that* string." A gravelly Scottish voice came out of nowhere.

Sam and J.J. screamed. Sam felt J.J.'s hand grip harder. Her eyes had adjusted, and she saw that bare, low-watt light bulbs with pull strings had replaced the fluorescents.

"Who's there?" Sam croaked.

A tall, slim man with a dark, curvy moustache emerged from the shadows. He held an odd-looking flashlight in one hand, though it was turned off. "Mr. Watt. At your service."

Sam's eyes widened. The hallway had definitely changed from where they'd started. Now, it was long and narrow, with a low ceiling.

J.J. jumped as a strange hissing sound came from behind Mr. Watt. She mumbled out of the side of her mouth to Sam. "What's going on? Where are we?"

Sam shrugged and sidled closer to J.J. She whispered, "Did you hear his name? I think he might be the old gardener."

J.J. gasped. "Oh, no. Then he *is* a ghost."

"Something else is really weird about where we are." Sam swallowed hard.

The man's voice had a Scottish lilt, like their neighbour who lived down the street. Although he was dressed in a crisp, pale-blue-and-white striped shirt, with a tie and a black vest, the knees of his dark pants were smudged with dirt. The chain of a watch glinted from his vest pocket.

"You little...ah, lasses..." A look of confusion fell across his face as he looked down at their jeans and brightly-coloured sneakers. "You must have come to see my special fungi crop."

Mr. Watt nodded to the open doorway nearby. A strange, earthy smell wafted over them. He stepped into the room and said, "Follow me."

J.J. held back and whispered to Sam, "The gardener grew mushrooms here years ago. How come everything is so real now?"

Sam squeezed her arm. "I don't know."

"You lasses will have to step inside if you want to see properly," called Mr. Watt.

"What are we going to do?" J.J. whispered.

"Let's go along with him and see if we can figure something out," Sam suggested.

J.J. clung to Sam as they stepped into the almost dark room. Only a tiny red light glowed from one corner of the ceiling.

"Smells like a barn in here," J.J. whispered. "It reminds me of my great Aunt Marsha's potato bin in the spring – mouldy, with rotting spuds."

Sam wrinkled her nose at the damp, musty smell. She could see three levels of wide, shallow, wooden boxes stretching from one wall to another. The air was misty and the hissing sounded again.

She and J.J. gave each other wide-eyed looks.

"Steam heat," Mr. Watt said, as he smoothed his moustache to either side of his face. His mouth held a hint of a smile. He gazed at the boxes filled with moist dirt and flecked with white, like a black sweater with bits of fluff on it. "The top berth of mushrooms will be ready for harvesting soon," he said.

Sam nodded, trying to remember what they'd learned on one of their previous trips to Government House.

"If you're still here in two or three days, you'll get to see the mushrooms pop through the ground." He frowned slightly. "Though this is not the place where most of His Honour Amédée Forget's guests like to dally."

"Oh no..." J.J. whispered. "Amédée Forget hasn't lived at Government House since 1910."

Sam started to respond. "Ah, we were, ah, that is we aren't, uh..." Her voice trailed off. Where *were* they?

Mr. Watt raised his eyebrows at them.

J.J. recovered first. "We aren't actually, well, we really aren't His Honour Amédée Forget's guests," she said in a low voice.

"You'll have to speak up if you want me to hear," Mr. Watt rubbed his left ear. "Sounded like you said you weren't His Honour's guests." He stared hard at them.

"We *are* visitors to Government House," Sam said. What if Mr. Watt asked them to leave? Would they be able to find their way back to their own time?

He nodded. "That's all right then."

"Wh-what was your name again?" J.J. asked.

"Mr. George Watt, head gardener here since 1894." He gave a slight bow of his head.

Sam's fingers grasped J.J.'s arm. No doubt about it. George Watt *was* a ghost. Mushrooms hadn't been grown in the stately home for decades. How could their surroundings seem so real? It was nothing like the ghost encounters they'd had before.

"Have we gone back in time?" Sam hissed at J.J.

"We'd better get back...uh, upstairs," J.J. said. Sam bobbed her head in agreement.

George Watt pulled out his pocket watch and checked the time. "A little early for noon break," he said. He stood polishing the cover. "But I expect you have other things to do."

"What a nice watch," said Sam, when she caught a glint of silver.

He held up the watch. She and J.J. leaned closer to look at the intricate design etched onto the silver.

"It was a parting gift from the duchess, who I worked for before coming to Canada," he said, as he tucked the watch carefully back into his vest pocket.

"Where did you come from?" asked Sam.

"Scotland." He stowed the handkerchief in a pocket in his pants. "Now mind yourselves a few moments while I turn on the hall light so you can see your way." He glanced back at them. "Make sure to close the door tight. Don't want to have any light leaking into the room. Mushrooms need darkness."

Sam and J.J. stood inside the doorway, their heads poking out as George Watt switched on his flashlight. He started down the dark hall.

"Wonder what year it is?" Sam kept her voice low.

"1903, though why you wouldn't know this begs a serious question." Mr. Watt had an odd sound to his voice as he turned to face them.

"We're just, uh, being silly," said Sam with an embarrassed-looking grin. His hearing seemed to have suddenly improved.

J.J. broke in. "How long have you been growing mushrooms?"

"This is the fifth year now." As if doubting their math skills, he added, "That would be since 1898."

"That's a very long time," said Sam. She stepped into the hallway, with J.J. right behind her. "You are obviously very good at it."

Mr. Watt smiled at her praise, and then continued down the hall.

"How are we going to get back to the others?" J.J. turned a worried face to Sam.

"Just go through the door that brought you here," George Watt pointed.

At the same time as he yanked on the light string, Sam whispered, "No one will ever believe we've been back in time with George Watt."

Instantly, Mr. Watt disappeared. And so did the hallway.

Sam and J.J. found themselves in a totally different room. In the dark. Silence. No hissing. No smell of dirt.

"What happened?" J.J. gasped.

"I think we flipped in time again!" Sam shivered. "How did we do that? And where are we now?" Sam spun around, and then moved closer to J.J.

"I have no idea." J.J. cowered tight to Sam.

They stared towards a streak of light that seeped around the cracks of a door. Their eyes adjusted to find a clutter of old, discarded furniture. From far away, they heard the sounds of their schoolmates' chattering.

"At least we seem to be in our own time." J.J. shuddered.

"Let's get out of here," Sam said, as she and J.J. grabbed hands and made for the outline of the door.

They tripped and clattered around stacks of chairs, small tables and other bits of furniture, swiping at cobwebs and sneezing at dust. Sam tugged on the doorknob, but it was stuck. J.J. gave it another yank.

Yes! It opened. By the time they ran down the hallway

to the bottom of the main staircase, they were breathing hard. They were just in time to see the last of their classmates disappear around the corner at the top of the stairs.

J.J. clung to the banister, trying to catch her breath.

Beside her, Sam gasped. "Not only did we see a ghost, but we actually went back into his time!"

J.J. shook her head. "I'm not sure I like this ghost-detecting business anymore."

"It was a little strange." Sam started laughing. "But can you imagine the look on Mr. Watt's face when we disappeared?"

J.J. giggled. "He was probably more surprised than we were."

They laughed harder, clinging to one another until they were weak. They sat on the bottom step and wiped the tears from their eyes.

Suddenly, the lights went out around them.

"No!" said Sam. "This can't be happening again."

Sam bolted up the carpeted staircase, with J.J. on her heels.

CHAPTER TWO

"THOUGHT THAT WOULD bring you girls up from wherever you were *not* supposed to be in the basement," said Mrs. Lindstrom with a frown. "Now stay with the class, or it'll be extra homework for the two of you."

She turned the light back on and strode to the front of the class in the reception area of the main foyer of the Queen Elizabeth II Wing.

J.J. and Sam joined the end of the ragged line of students. Everyone was talking and admiring their posters. Mrs. Lindstrom passed theirs along the line toward them.

"Too bad you girls didn't get much done on yours. You'll have to make up the time after school," she said.

Their class assignment was to create posters for a provincial contest celebrating a special anniversary of the opening of Government House.

"Yuck." Sam started to crumple hers up.

"Wait." J.J. grabbed her friend's hands. Sam was always so impatient. "You get class marks for doing it, even if you don't enter the contest. Besides, it's not bad."

Sam grimaced and smoothed out her poster. "I guess we have to get all the marks we can."

"And stay on the good side of Mrs. Lindstrom too." J.J.

nudged Sam forward. They pushed past the other students, jostling for positions right at the front of the disorderly line.

"Are there any last questions for our visitor experience host, Robin?" Mrs. Lindstrom asked.

J.J.'s hand shot up. "What can you tell us about Mr. Watt growing mushrooms?"

Mrs. Lindstrom raised an eyebrow in annoyance.

"When our class came last year, you told us he grew them where the activity room is now," Sam said.

"Right. I thought that when I first started working here." Robin grinned. "But I was mistaken. He actually grew the mushrooms under the current ballroom. That's where the old conservatory used to be."

"So what's under the room now?" asked J.J. She wanted to make sure they were talking about the same place.

"The furnace room, maintenance areas, storage rooms with old furniture, and things like that," Robin said. "Several sections and rooms have changed over the years, with old parts of the building being torn down, and new ones being built."

J.J. gave a sideways glance at Sam. That explained how they ended up in a storage room when they shifted back to the present time. But what triggered them going to the past in the first place? And how had they gotten back?

Robin continued. "I've been studying more about the residence, and there used to be all kinds of buildings on the grounds too."

"Like what?" J.J. asked.

One of her classmates groaned behind her.

"We'll never get out of here now," grumbled another.

Scuffling and chattering erupted, along with beeps and rings from cellphones.

J.J. ignored her classmates, while Mrs. Lindstrom asked everyone to settle down and put away their cell phones until they were outside. J.J. and Sam listened keenly.

"Stables, the carriage house, the gardener's cottage and the staff quarters." Robin pointed towards the west. "They were all on that side of the residence. A couple of summers ago, someone found a small piece of the foundation of the building where the staff lived."

"Could we go see?" J.J. asked.

Mrs. Lindstrom interrupted. "Not today, girls!"

"Besides, I don't know where they were exactly," Robin said. "We have a few ideas where all the buildings were, but the research hasn't been completed on that. There isn't too much information available."

"Aw, too bad," J.J. said.

"Is there someone around who knows about the olden days?" Sam asked.

"And about what went on here then?" J.J. said.

"There is a resident next door at Pioneer Village who was on staff here when she was younger," Robin said. "She might be able to tell you what it was like to work here fifty or sixty years ago. She might have heard stories about the older times as well."

"Great! Could we go see her?" Sam asked.

Mrs. Lindstrom lifted her eyes to the ceiling and shook her head. She seemed to be counting to ten silently.

Before she could speak, Robin cut in. "I'm sure you could visit her, but you'd have to make an appointment ahead of time."

"And it would have to be after school hours," said Mrs. Lindstrom, looking relieved. "Let's go, girls, it's almost lunch time."

A chorus of kids took up a chant. "We're hungry!"

"Let's leave the history nerds behind," one snippy girl said.

Sam scowled at her classmates.

"Can you tell us...?" J.J. started to ask.

"Her name is Mrs. Alice Goudy. Just call the main number at Pioneer Village and ask if you can talk to her," Robin said.

Mrs. Lindstrom didn't wait for Sam or J.J. to ask anything else. "That's all the time we have for questions. Let's give a big Wascana School show of appreciation for Robin."

Everyone clapped. J.J. and Sam were the loudest.

As the group moved towards the exit, Sam and J.J. hung back, letting their classmates pass them.

J.J. shifted her poster and held it by the corners to keep it flat.

"Let's visit Mrs. Goudy as soon as possible and see what she knows."

Sam nodded in agreement. "I'll call her right after school. Maybe she'll know something about Mr. Watt too."

"Seeing him was even more amazing than seeing the other ghosts," J.J. said.

"Yeah, going back to his time was awesome."

"But how did it happen?" J.J. gave Sam a puzzled look.

"And will it happen again?" Sam asked.

J.J. and Sam both glanced over their shoulders toward the ballroom. J.J. tried to envision the conservatory and the basement beneath it all those years ago.

"I hope that it does, so we can find out more." Sam flashed J.J. a mischievous smile.

"But what if we couldn't get back home?" J.J. turned a worried face to Sam. "I'm not sure how we got back to the present just now."

"First, we have to find out how to get there again," Sam said.

No thanks, J.J. thought. She gave a little shiver. "Come on, we'd better catch up to the others before we miss the bus back to school, and Mrs. Lindstrom gives us more homework, after all."

JUST AFTER SIX P.M. that evening, Sam popped next door to collect J.J. for their visit to Mrs. Goudy.

"It's starting to get dark. Do you have your cell phone?" Sam heard J.J.'s dad ask as her friend stepped outside. It was autumn, and the air was chilly.

"Right here in my backpack, Dad," J.J. assured him.

"I have mine too, Mr. Forbes," Sam called back to him. "One of my parents will come to meet us for the walk home." Pioneer Village was only four blocks away.

"Okay. Have fun, girls." Mr. Forbes appeared at the door and watched them walk off.

"We're lucky Mrs. Goudy could see us so soon," Sam said. "She's usually busy with her quilting group, but they had to cancel tonight. She sure was excited by our visit when I called."

"Too bad we had soccer practice after school," J.J said.

Sam glanced up at the darkening sky. The edge of the

full harvest moon was already bright on the horizon.
"Yeah. Otherwise, we could have gone while it was still
daylight."

They crossed Dewdney Avenue and stepped through
the iron gateway onto the Government House grounds, a
short-cut to the seniors' complex. They scuffled across to
the paved walkway, their sneakers sending up the scent
of dust and dry grass. An occasional waft of air whirled
fallen leaves in front of them, as they walked along the
curved path through the dying flower gardens.

"Hope she's nice like Grandma Louise," Sam said. She
hadn't seen her favourite grandmother for over three
months.

"Where is your grandma now?" J.J asked.

"Gram's decided to travel on a river cruise. She's
made it as far as Vienna, according to the last postcard
she sent us," Sam said. "She's not coming back from
Europe for another couple of months." Sam shook her
head. "She won't be able to help us with our ghost problems
this time."

"Gosh, you're right. But I know how much you miss
your gram for other reasons besides that," J.J. said. "Even
though mine is only in Moose Jaw, I don't get to see her
often enough either."

Sam felt a lurch in her stomach as she thought about
how much J.J. missed her mom since she passed away
from cancer almost a year before. J.J.'s grandmother was
the only family link left to her mom, outside of her dad.

"Do you expect your grandmother to visit any time
soon?" Sam asked.

"No. Since Dad started his new job, he doesn't have
to travel so much, so Grandma doesn't have to stay with

me anymore."

"But now your dad should have more time to take you to see her," suggested Sam.

J.J. shook her head. "Dad's working on an important project, so that means he doesn't have much time to visit her. But at least he can do some of his work at home, so he's there with me more."

Sam turned excitedly to J.J. "Maybe he could help us find out where the old buildings were at Government House."

J.J. giggled. "He's an architect, not an archivist, or archaeologist."

"Still, he knows about buildings." Sam felt her face turn red. She didn't want to admit to J.J. that she still didn't really know what an architect did.

"Let's hurry, it's getting dark fast." J.J. shot forward at a quicker pace.

Although occasional lamp posts glowed along the paths through the Government House grounds, the large evergreens cast long, solid shadows. The elms and other trees, barren of leaves, were scratchy against the almost-dark sky. The odd shapes of bushes looked like people crouching. Hedges seemed like prime places for lurkers to hide.

Sam and J.J. clung together as they followed a curve halfway across the grounds. Somewhere to the left of a flower bed, the tinkling laughter of several people floated in the night air. They stopped in their tracks.

"Who's there?" asked J.J. in a whisper. As soon as she spoke, the laughter stopped.

Sam and J.J. peered across the grounds.

"Do you see anyone?" J.J. murmured.

"No, but I'm sure we're not alone." Sam felt her pulse quicken.

"This is creepy," J.J. said.

They ran the rest of the way.

CHAPTER THREE

SAM BREATHED HARD with relief when they arrived at the well-lit entrance of the seniors' home. J.J. gasped for breath beside her.

A few minutes later, they entered the foyer. A young woman with a purple-streaked bob and one dangling earring greeted them at the reception desk. Her name tag read "Amber." Sam told her why they'd come.

"Mrs. Goudy is waiting for you in her suite." Amber dipped her head. "I'll take you to her."

Sam and J.J. followed Amber down a series of hallways. As they rounded a corner, J.J. came to a full stop, and Sam bumped into her.

"Who is that?" J.J. whispered to Sam.

Sam looked ahead and saw a woman with short, curly hair standing in the hall several metres ahead of them. She was dressed in a flared, blue flowered dress that was belted at the waist, and her head was tilted to one side, as if she was observing them.

"Is that Mrs. Goudy?" Sam asked Amber.

Amber looked confused. "Is who Mrs. Goudy?"

"The lady right in front of us," J.J. said. She smiled at the woman, who looked strangely familiar.

Amber gave them an odd look. "There isn't anyone there."

"She's right...uh," J.J. stopped. The woman had disappeared.

"Uh, she's gone now," said Sam, wondering where she'd gone so fast.

"I guess I missed seeing her." Amber shrugged. "But it's odd because I thought everyone in this wing was down at bingo tonight." She led them to the end of the hall.

As they trailed behind, J.J. mouthed the word "ghost" to Sam, who nodded.

"Could be," she mouthed back.

Sam and J.J. almost walked into Amber as she stopped at the first door on their right.

Amber knocked and opened the door to a cheery, "come in." She stood aside to reveal a comfortable room with doily-adorned furniture. Sam and J.J. greeted the slender, white-haired woman who sat across from them in a puffy, reclining armchair. Beside Mrs. Goudy, a folded walker rested next to a wall that was covered with framed photographs of people from a long time ago.

"Thank you, Amber. Come in, girls." Mrs. Goudy stretched out her hands. "I'm delighted to meet you," she said, grabbing a hand from each of them. Her brown eyes sparkled, and a slight dimple appeared on one cheek. "Please, be seated."

She swept her arm in a theatrical gesture towards a rose-coloured love seat next to her armchair. Her white hair was swept up in a twist on the top of her head, and her graceful movements reminded Sam of an olden-day movie star.

Sam and J.J. sank into the love seat beside one another.

"Can I offer you some juice before we get started?" Mrs. Goudy started to rise and reach for her walker.

"I can get that for you, Mrs. G.," Amber said.

"If it wouldn't be too much trouble, I would appreciate it." Mrs. Goudy beamed up at her.

"Sure thing, Mrs. G.," Amber said.

"Apple or cranberry, dears?" Mrs. Goudy raised her eyebrows at the girls.

When they'd made their selection and Amber had stepped away into the small kitchen, Mrs. Goudy relaxed with her hands on her lap. "Now, tell me girls, which one of you phoned me?"

Sam waved her hand.

"You must be Sam, then." Her eyes lit up. "And you would be J.J.?" She turned her smile on J.J. "I have to say that you two look familiar, like I've met you somewhere before."

"I don't think so," Sam said. J.J. shook her head.

"Just my mind playing tricks." Mrs. Goudy leaned a little bit forward. "Well then, how may I be of help? Was it posters, you said?"

"Yes, the posters are supposed to show something about Government House over the last 125 years," Sam explained. "They're for a school project, and also to enter a provincial contest."

"Oh, yes, I remember you mentioned it was for an anniversary celebration," Mrs. Goudy said. "I'm not sure how much help I can be, but I'll give it a whirl. What did you need to know, specifically?"

"For my poster, I'd like to know what the grounds and buildings were like a long time ago," Sam said. She drew her notebook and pen from her backpack.

J.J. added, "We'd also like to know what it was like when you worked at Government House, and about some of the others who worked there."

Mrs. Goudy nodded. "My sister and I worked together for a time in the late 1930s and into the early 1940s."

"You must have been really young then," J.J. said.

"Bless you child, aren't you sweet." Mrs. Goudy's cheery laugh rang out. "I'm afraid I'm actually rather older than you think."

"You don't look very old," said Sam, thinking Mrs. Goudy looked full of fun, like her own grandmother.

"I'll leave you two to figure out my age from what I tell you," she said, with a mischievous twinkle in her eyes.

Amber returned with their juices and set them on hand-crocheted doilies on a round coffee table, next to a bright bouquet of fall flowers. Sam murmured her thanks and took a tiny sip. She and J.J. set their glasses back down at the same time.

"What do you remember most about working at Government House?" asked J.J.

"Where shall I start?" Mrs. Goudy said with a tinkling laugh. "We had such grand times in those days. His Honour Archibald McNab was living there then. He had a wonderful sense of humour, so down to earth. He wanted us all to call him Archie, but of course, that wasn't proper."

Mrs. Goudy clasped her hands. Her face held a faraway look as she continued. "Even though there were hard economic times in the 1930s and during the Second World War, the house was filled with important people coming to visit – royalty, movie stars. We just made do with our limited provisions. Mrs. McNab was such a dear too, always coming up with sensible ideas to make everything stretch and seem elegant at the same time."

"Who were some of the special people who visited?" Sam asked with pen poised. She took a long sip of her apple juice and glanced at J.J., who was scanning the room.

"King George VI and Queen Elizabeth in 1939. Before they arrived, the house was redecorated in delicate creams and lavenders. It was simply beautiful, and the royals were so delightful." Mrs. Goudy settled back in her chair. "And then there were the movie stars from the Hollywood blockbuster *North West Mounted Police* – Madeleine Carroll and Robert Preston. Oh my, he was handsome, and she was so lovely and smart."

Sam shot a puzzled look at J.J., who shrugged.

"We don't know those movie stars or the movie," J.J. said. She took a drink from her cranberry juice.

"Of course you wouldn't, dears. Though the film really was very good at the time," Mrs. Goudy said.

"Who else was working there then?" Sam asked. She leaned her notebook on the plump arm of the couch, pen ready. J.J. sat back.

"George Cooke was the janitor and did house maintenance – we stayed friends until his death about ten years ago. Then there were the two gardeners. Ernie Myles looked after the grounds, and J.P. Dewey managed the greenhouse. Bert was the chauffeur."

She paused for Sam to finish writing the names down.

"And then, in the house, there was Ruby, who was the secretary and companion to Mrs. McNab. My sister Lily and I were housemaids. I did the upstairs bedrooms and the laundry. She did the downstairs. You'll see some pictures of them all in my rogues' gallery."

She pointed to a few photographs with various groups of the staff standing outside on the grounds in front of a hedge.

"There's Howie," said Sam. He was on the edge of a group of people, partly cut off. She knew it was the only known photo of him.

Turning to Mrs. Goudy, J.J. added, "We learned about him on a different research project."

"Did you know him?" Sam asked, suddenly remembering he had been the cook during Mr. McNab's time. She exchanged looks with J.J. They'd met him as a ghost on their previous visits to Government House.

Mrs. Goudy looked puzzled. "There was no one by the name of Howie that I recall. That's Cheun Lee."

Sam tapped her hand to her forehead, as she remembered that the name "Howie" was only given to the cook after he had started haunting the building.

Mrs. Goudy continued. "He died before I arrived. My sister knew him a little, though. I kept her copy of the photo because it has some of the staff I knew too."

Sam asked, "Did she tell you anything about him?"

"Not really, just that he was separated from his wife and family. He used to send money back to them in China. He suffered from insomnia – not being able to sleep through the night – so he'd shuffle back and forth down the halls in his slippers."

That tallied with what Sam and J.J already knew. He'd sure scared them when they heard him walk right through a wall one night when they had been at Government House.

"Have you heard the ghost stories about Government

House?" J.J. asked.

Mrs. Goudy shook her head and cleared her throat. "Now about the other staff. The cook hired after Cheun Lee was Katherine Sauer – Kate. She also helped me with the laundry. And she was a very good cook."

Mrs. Goudy turned a bright smile on them. "And I remember this wonderful ceramic tile floor in the kitchen. It was so easy to keep clean. But not so good if you dropped a dish, which I did from time to time when I helped serve. I was more useful making beds, dusting and doing floors than helping in the kitchen." Mrs. Goudy shrugged her shoulders. "Some of us are just better at some things than others."

"Like J.J. is at drawing," Sam said. "Any art projects I do aren't very good, especially the poster we have to do for the Government House Anniversary."

Mrs. Goudy tilted her head towards Sam. "I've always believed that doing your best is all you can do. It's the attempt that's important, not always the outcome."

Sam didn't feel confident about her attempts either. "My drawings of the buildings from the past aren't very exciting," she sighed. "There are hardly any photos of them."

"I'm sure you'll do fine with it."

A sudden brain wave struck Sam. "What if I included the people from the past who worked at Government House? Maybe do a photo-collage of them over a plan of the grounds, with the old buildings?" She brightened and glanced at J.J., who gave her the thumbs up.

Sam leaned towards Mrs. Goudy with her hands clasped. "Could I maybe get copies of some of your old photos?"

Mrs. Goudy looked thoughtful for a few moments. "I believe that should be possible. When do you need them?"

"I have to hand in my poster at the end of the week, so there's not much time." Sam gave Mrs. Goudy what she thought was an apologetic, yet hopeful look.

"Let me ask Amber if she can make copies for you. I'll get back to you by tomorrow evening."

Sam scribbled her phone number on a sheet from her notebook, tore it off, and handed it to the elderly woman.

"Now, who else do you need to know about?" Mrs. Goudy asked.

"Do you know anything about some of the earlier staff?" J.J. asked. "Like the gardener who grew the mushrooms?"

Mrs. Goudy laughed. "George Watt was quite a bit before my time, but he certainly was known for his landscaping and gardening around Government House and the Legislative Buildings. But then, you probably already knew that, right?"

J.J. and Sam nodded.

"I bet you didn't know he planted caragana bushes at Government House – the first caragana to grow in Regina soil."

Sam and J.J. shook their heads. "What's caragana?" Sam asked.

"Wonderful bushes that grow quickly," Mrs. Goudy said. "Almost everyone used to have them as borders in their yards. Now you mostly see them in small towns or on farmyards. In the spring they have little yellow flowers, and when we were children, we used to eat them. They're in all the outdoor staff pictures." She nodded towards her wall.

"*That's* what those hedges must be in the park across from your grandmother's in Moose Jaw," Sam said.

"I didn't know that's what they were called," J.J. said.

Mrs. Goudy continued. "When the King and Queen were here in 1939, they were so enthralled with the caragana hedges that Mr. McNab gave them some seedlings to take back to England. At that time, caragana hedges surrounded the mansion and went down past the houses for the gardener and coachman."

J.J. leaned towards Mrs. Goudy. "Where were the other buildings on the property?"

"I'd especially like to know more about where the staff lived," Sam said.

"The buildings were all west of the big house," Mrs. Goudy said. She took the notebook and pencil that Sam offered and drew a little sketch of where the buildings had been. The girls studied it while Mrs. Goudy continued talking.

"There's nothing left there now that I know of. Ernie Myles lived in the gardener's cottage, which, as you can see, was in a direct line with the current conservatory on the edge of the present property. I used to walk across the yard from the staff's quarters to visit him on his porch in the summer evenings once I was off work." She gave a little sigh.

"He was like an older brother to my sister and me, though Lily preferred to spend her time with the chauffeur. Bert Timmons was more her age, but he only lived on the grounds for a short time. The coachman's house wasn't the greatest and ended up being used for storage." Mrs. Goudy shifted in her recliner. "Lily was three years older than I was, and Bert took her to the movies on a

Saturday night. Until she found out he showed interest in someone else at the same time. That romance ended in a hurry," she said with regret.

"But before that, we all went to the world premiere of the movie *North West Mounted Police*. It was shown at the Capital Theatre right here in Regina, on Monday, October 21, 1940."

"How can you remember the exact date?" J.J. asked with surprise.

"We went the day before my nineteenth birthday. What fun we had that night!"

Mrs. Goudy pointed to a small, framed black and white photograph on the wall beside her. "There's the picture of us with the actress in front of the movie theatre. Ernie came with Lily, Bert and me."

Sam and J.J. leaned over her shoulder to see four young people gathered around a woman in a long, sparkly evening gown, with a fur stole. Her long, blonde hair flowed in waves past her shoulders, as she snuggled close to Bert. Bert had a huge grin on his face, as he leaned towards the movie star. A young woman with short, curly, dark hair had her arm linked with Bert's. The picture was so small it was hard to tell, but she seemed to have a forced smile on her face that was half-turned towards him.

"The actress looks friendly." Sam stared at the photo.

"You could say that," laughed Mrs. Goudy. "She took a real shine to Bert. After that night, he used to write her letters, and she'd send him autographed photographs." Mrs. Goudy shook her head. "Of course, it all came to nothing. What would a Hollywood movie star want with a chauffeur in another country? It was just a lark for her, really, and didn't mean anything." She spread her hands and shrugged her shoulders. "But by the time Bert figured out that he'd made a terrible mistake when my sister dropped him, she had met someone else."

Sam jumped up. "Who are those people?" She pointed to the top row of photographs.

J.J. joined Sam to look more closely. Some photographs were much older than the others. A few were brownish, some were black-and-white, and several were old square photos with faded colours.

"These are photos of my family as far back as I have them," Mrs. Goudy said. "The other people on the far left are staff from when I worked at Government House."

Sam went to look at the photos of the staff, while J.J. continued to study the family ones.

"Who's that?" J.J. asked about the photograph slightly below the others. A laughing light-haired young man in a uniform stood beside a caragana hedge.

"Just one of the temporary summer groundskeepers," Mrs. Goudy murmured. "I don't even recall his name now." She turned away.

J.J. SHARED A LOOK of disbelief with Sam. Why would Mrs. Goudy have a photograph of someone whose name she didn't remember on her wall? She must know who he was, but why didn't she want to tell them?

Mrs. Goudy had gone silent, her face sad.

To fill the awkward moment, J.J. blurted out the first thing that came to mind. "The styles in dresses sure have changed."

"Indeed," said Mrs. Goudy. Her face brightened again. "You can tell the era by what the women wore." She pointed out how the hemlines went higher and the skirts tighter as the decades passed. "Men's clothing is harder to pinpoint in time, because it doesn't change as much."

J.J. recalled the clothing that George Watt had worn when they'd met him. The vest with the pocket watch was a dead giveaway that he was from the past, but otherwise they wouldn't have known.

Mrs. Goudy pointed to another photo. "There I am with my husband, Edward." A tall, dark-haired man stood with his arm around his young bride's waist and a shy, happy smile on his face.

J.J. didn't recognize their Mrs. Goudy, except for her charming smile and the little dimple on her cheek. Otherwise, the young woman in the photo, with her wavy blonde hairstyle and 1940s clothing, bore no resemblance to the woman in the room with them.

J.J. noticed another photo nearby, of two young women standing in front of a caragana hedge with their arms around each other's waists.

She gasped. "Is that you with your sister?"

"Yes, just before Lily left to be married in 1941, and not to Bert." Mrs. Goudy looked sad. "He didn't stay working there more than a few months after the movie night photo was taken."

"Sam, look at this one."

The woman beside Alice Goudy was the woman they'd seen in the hallway – and she was wearing the same flared, flowered dress, belted at the waist! Though the photo was in black and white, there was no mistaking the same pattern on the dress.

Sam stepped over to look. "Oh, wow."

"What is it?" Mrs. Goudy asked, clearly surprised by their interest.

J.J. murmured, "She looks like someone we've...uh... seen before."

Suddenly, J.J.'s heart thumped. This woman looked suspiciously like the one from the previous day in the basement of Government House! She'd have to remember to tell Sam about her.

"I don't think you could have." Mrs. Goudy shook her head.

"Is she still...uh...alive?" Sam asked.

"Why no." Mrs. Goudy stared at her. "Lily passed away fairly young – only a couple of years after she married. Not long after that picture was taken, in fact. Why do you ask?"

Sam looked at J.J. for help.

J.J. didn't know what to say. The woman they'd seen in the hall was a ghost. But how could they explain that to Mrs. Goudy? J.J. thought fast. "There don't seem to be any photos of her when she's older."

"At least not that we've seen," Sam added, as she moved back to the love seat.

"You two are very sharp." Mrs. Goudy smiled, but she didn't give them any details about her sister's death.

"You and your sister look quite a bit alike, except for the different hair colours," J.J. said. She studied the photographs for a few more moments, sneaking looks at Sam. They needed to talk. Mrs. Goudy seemed to be lost in thought.

Suddenly J.J. felt something cold, like an icy hand, touch her shoulder. There was no one beside her. As she shook the feeling off, a shiver ran up the full length of her back. She decided not to say anything.

From the other side of the room, a pendulum clock chimed eight times.

"I guess we have to head home now." Sam gathered up her notebook and pen to stuff them into her backpack.

"Just leave the glasses, dear," Mrs. Goudy said, as J.J. bent to pick them up. "Amber will collect them for me. She's good that way."

"Thank you so much for letting us visit," Sam said.

"The pleasure has been all mine. I'll telephone you when I have the photographs ready," said Mrs. Goudy. "It's wonderful to talk about the past with someone who is interested. Please come again, any time." Her eyes shone as they said their goodbyes and left.

Once they reached the reception area, Amber waved goodbye and headed down the hall. J.J. watched her turn the corner towards Mrs. Goudy's room.

J.J. felt a sudden waft of cold air. As she turned back towards Sam, J.J. did a double take.

Out of the corner of her eye, J.J. was sure she'd seen a translucent figure of a woman down the hall. The same woman as in the photo - Lily! Before J.J. had time to say anything to Sam, Lily held a finger to her lips, as if asking her not to say a word. Then, she vanished.

Sam was busy on her cell phone. "We're leaving now, Mom." A pause. "Okay, meet you at the corner. Bye."

Sam grabbed J.J.'s hand and pulled her outside. "We have to hurry. Mom's a fast walker."

Running breathlessly beside her, J.J. didn't have a chance to tell Sam what had happened.

J.J. and Sam raced across the two parking lots and

down the moonlit path through the Government House grounds. As they hurried around the bend where they'd heard the laughter earlier, J.J. paused, but there was no disturbance in the night air. Once they reached the rose gardens near the main entrance, they slowed to a walk.

"I'd like to know why Mrs. Goudy pretended not to know the name of the man in the photo," Sam said.

"Maybe he's an old boyfriend," J.J. suggested with a giggle.

"I bet Mrs. Goudy knows something about the ghosts at Government House too," Sam said.

"I wonder why she didn't want to talk about it," J.J. said.

"Maybe if we visit her again, she'll tell us more," Sam said.

"I'd like to know more about her sister too." J.J. told Sam about the icy hand on her shoulder, and what she'd seen before they'd left. "I hope we get a chance to see her again. I'd like to know why she wanted me to keep quiet about seeing her."

"Maybe we will when we go back to pick up my photos for the poster," Sam suggested.

"I wonder why we keep running into ghosts even when we're not looking for them," J.J. said.

"Yeah, everything to do with Government House seems to be haunted," Sam said.

"And now Pioneer Village too," J.J. said.

"Must be because Mrs. Goudy has the connection to Government House, with all those photos up, and her sister probably stays close to her too."

J.J. stopped and gazed up. A full harvest moon glowed golden against the crisp navy sky. J.J. gazed at it for a few moments. Sam stood beside her, staring into the night. There was a gentle hint of wind, but otherwise, even the sound of the distant traffic was muted.

"It's so beautiful," J.J. said. "I wish I could paint what I'm seeing."

"Let's take a picture." Sam pointed her cell phone at the sky and snapped. She looked at the result. "Not so good."

"Never mind. Let's not be late to meet your mom," J.J. said.

Sam hissed at her suddenly. "What's that?"

J.J.'s eyes followed where Sam pointed. J.J. scanned the shadow-laden foliage of the grounds, staring in turn at bushes, pathways, and flower garden mounds. A caragana bush seemed to have materialized where one hadn't been before. And at its edge was a human-like shape.

"Is that a person?" Sam whispered.

"I can't tell if it's anything." J.J. moved closer to Sam.

Sam raised her cell phone. "I'll take a photo, and then maybe we will be able to see."

"If the shape is a person, the flash should temporarily blind him, and give us time to run," J.J. said. If it was a ghost, she didn't have any idea what would happen, but maybe they'd have a photo of it.

Heart pounding, J.J. held her breath as Sam raised her camera. The shape separated from the bushes.

J.J. jerked Sam's arm. The flash went off.

"Come on!" J.J. turned and ran.

Sam raced after her.

J.J. didn't dare look back.

What was lurking in the bushes? Was it a person, or was it a ghost?

J.J. didn't know, and she wasn't sticking around to find out. She sprinted behind Sam, across the street to where Sam's mother waited for them under the lamplight, hoping they'd left whatever it was far behind them.

CHAPTER FOUR

THE NEXT DAY, AFTER school soccer practice, J.J. and Sam hurried along the two blocks to Government House. With only half an hour to explore the grounds, they didn't want to waste any time before they had to return home for supper and to work on their posters.

The late afternoon was turning to twilight as they crossed into the mansion grounds through the northwest service gate. Leaves crunched underfoot, and frost nipped the air.

"Too bad that photo you took last night wasn't any good," J.J. snickered. "Not even a good shot of the sky." The picture ended up being an angle shot of black, with a blob of light from the flash.

"At least it scared off whoever was there," Sam said, shrugging her shoulders.

"Luckily, there's still some light right now, and we can see there's no one here," J.J. said. She adjusted her backpack that held a flashlight, measuring tape and notebook.

Sam said, "I'm sure we can find something to show us where the buildings might have been."

"Robin did say there was a strip of foundation out here somewhere," J.J. said.

Sam secured her dad's camera around her neck and unfolded Mrs. Goudy's hand-drawn diagram. "This should help, though things must have changed over the years since she worked here."

Together they studied the landscape and compared it to the drawing, then headed across the grounds. Gusts of wind whipped their hair, and they pulled their hoodies tighter around their necks. The fading light cast shadows across patches of lawn, making it difficult to see details.

Beyond the last flower bed, J.J. switched on the flashlight. All was quiet except for the wind hustling leaves along the ground.

"I'm not sure it was a good idea to come out here right now." J.J. shivered. "It's kind of creepy. Especially after last night."

"We'll be fast." Sam quickened her pace. J.J. rushed to keep up.

They consulted the sketch as they scoured the grass, weaving back and forth across the back of the grounds. Next to the property was a huge soccer field for the nearby high school, and, closer to Dewdney Ave, a church and its parking lot.

"The staff's quarters should be right around here somewhere." Sam poked at the ground with her toe.

J.J. crouched down to look across the lawn for rises or dips that might show where the building had stood, but except for the odd tree and clump of bushes, the area seemed flat. She jumped up and joined Sam again. They took slower, tinier steps, walking close beside each other.

All of a sudden, J.J.'s sneaker scuffed against something solid. "There it is."

She knelt down beside a narrow strip of broken concrete half-buried in the lawn. She smoothed the grass away from the edges.

"Wow, the foundation has sunk into the ground," J.J. said. "What's left of it." She dug around the strip with her pencil, but only found hard soil.

Sam crowded in beside J.J. "Great sleuthing!" She stood up and adjusted the camera. "Put your foot beside it, and I'll take a photo."

She whirred off several shots of the ground, and then took a couple facing towards Government House to help them find the sunken foundation again.

"Take some the other way too," suggested J.J. "I'll stay here." J.J. set her backpack on the ground.

Sam walked to the edge of the flower bed and snapped photographs towards J.J. As she headed back, she checked the images in the camera. "They're a little dark. We could fix them, but I'd rather we come back to take some in daylight."

J.J. glanced up at the waning moon that had risen and was half-hidden by bunching grey clouds. The grounds were shrouded by the dusk. She just wanted to get out of there, and fast!

"Let's see if there is any more of the foundation before we go," Sam said. "We can measure it when we come back." She slid her camera into J.J.'s backpack.

Sam slipped the map into her jacket pocket. "Maybe this was a corner," she said.

With a sigh, J.J. angled the flashlight toward the ground to shine at the end of the piece of foundation.

Sam said, "I'll walk at a right angle away from you. We'll count our footsteps to twenty-five, to start with."

They both stepped onto the narrow piece of concrete, clutching at each other to keep their balance.

Suddenly, the landscape wavered before their eyes.

"Jump off!" Sam yelled, yanking J.J.

They tumbled to the ground and rolled.

"Oh no," shrieked J.J.

Right where they had been standing was a two-storey building – *the staff quarters.*

"We've gone back in time again," Sam yelped. She helped J.J. scramble to her feet.

J.J. stared up at the wooden structure that towered before them, dark and foreboding. Above them, the stars were pinpricks in a cloudless night sky, and the moon had become a high globe of white.

J.J. stepped back, only to find a caragana hedge blocking their way. The hedge seemed to be sheltering the beginning of the wooden sidewalk that stretched towards the main mansion. The grounds extended to the west of the staff building for quite a distance before lights could be seen glinting from some houses.

"We're really in trouble this time." J.J. cowered beside Sam. "How will we ever get back?"

Sam put her arm around J.J. "Obviously we can't stand on the foundation piece again."

"No kidding, Sherlock," J.J. shivered. "So what *do* we do?"

"Let's head toward the gate. Maybe it's only the grounds that are back in time," suggested Sam.

J.J. looked around, but she couldn't see the gate. Everywhere she looked, she saw trees, bushes, and tall rows of caragana hedges.

"Sheesh, George Watt sure went crazy with planting

trees and hedges," J.J. said.

SUDDENLY, THE SKY brightened. It was broad daylight. In fact, it was a hot spring day, and everything was budding and turning green.

"Some might say I'm crazy," said a deep voice behind Sam. "I prefer to call it landscaping."

Sam and J.J. whirled around.

"We've shifted again," said Sam.

Sam stared at George Watt, kneeling in a tilled patch of dirt in front of them. He had a trowel in his hand and was planting seedlings from a wheelbarrow parked nearby. The smell of freshly dug earth and matted roots mingled with the scent of lilac blossoms from farther away.

Everywhere Sam and J.J. looked, the grounds stretched on forever. All the city streets, traffic, and houses were gone. Aside from the occasional planted tree and a few out-buildings around Government House, they were surrounded by open prairie, with only a few structures far off in the distance. The sun beat down on them.

Sam's heart raced. "I don't recognize anything."

"Me either," J.J. said. Her voice wavered.

"The North-West Mounted Police barracks are there," George said, noting their curiosity. "The Territorial Administrative Buildings are that way." He wiped the sweat from his face with a handkerchief, and then tucked it back into his pants pocket.

Sam stared at J.J. They had gone even farther back in time than they had moments before.

"It sure is empty out here," Sam said. "And hot." She unzipped her hoodie.

"Uh, gosh, I never expected to see anything like this," J.J. said. She tied her hoodie around her waist.

George smoothed his moustache and gazed over the grounds. "It'll be a few more years of work until I get this properly landscaped, with the tree plantations and all the flower beds growing well."

Sam saw several spots where flat stones had been laid around plots of cultivated earth. A few stray plants grew in each of them.

"There's the rose garden." Sam pointed to where two sticks stuck out of the dirt.

George looked at her in surprise. "How did you know that? They're nothing but twigs yet."

"Um, I just guessed," Sam sputtered. A rose garden grew in the same place in the present day.

"Looks like a good place to put one," J.J. said, with a little chuckle. "My dad just planted some roses too."

George squinted at them. He didn't seem entirely satisfied with their answers. "You two seem to turn up in the most unusual places."

Sam almost snorted. So did *he*!

J.J. whispered, "If he only knew."

"Do your hosts know you are out here?" George took his silver pocket watch from his vest pocket and checked it. "It's almost time for dinner."

He clicked the watch cover shut and polished it with his handkerchief. Gently, he replaced the watch in his vest pocket and patted his chest. "You'd best be getting back before the Forgets miss you."

Sam looked at J.J. again. She'd really like to get back –

to their time – but how were they supposed to do that?

"Uh, we're not exactly sure how to get there." Sam stumbled over the words.

George gave them another peculiar look. "Where did you say you come from again?"

"Uh. North, we uh, come from north of here," J.J. blurted.

Sam almost choked. "Ah, yes, right...from north of here." Only two blocks north, so they weren't lying, but gosh, their presence was tricky to explain.

George frowned at them and mumbled something about people with no sense of direction. Louder, he said, "Well, the Forgets don't like people to be late for meals, so you'd best skedaddle back to the main house over that way."

"Where's the wooden sidewalk?" Sam asked.

George opened his mouth, then closed it again, clearly puzzled. "I'm thinking you girls had best stay with your folks at the main house, if you can't find your way about here." He tilted his head at them. "Follow this furrow until you come to the house. If you get lost, just cut across the yard." He gave a little chuckle.

Sam cringed with embarrassment. There was nothing to obscure their path. No bushes, no wooden sidewalk. The main house was directly across the short prairie grass.

George continued, giving them patient instructions. "The housekeeper will let you in by the back entrance. Mind, you'll need to use the broom to clean the dust off your shoes before you go inside, or she'll be none too pleased. And you'll have to put on proper clothes for dinner."

As Sam and J.J. started off along the dirt path, George

called after them. "If you're lucky, you'll be served mush-rooms on toast. You missed coming back to see them pop up and be picked. There will be more poking through tomorrow, if you want to come and see. That is, if you can find your way back down to the basement," George said, not unkindly.

"We'll come if we can," J.J. called.

Sam waved goodbye.

"Great," Sam said. "Now he thinks we're not very smart."

"He may not be so wrong," said J.J. with a grimace. "We seem to be in 1903, *but* we don't know how to get back home."

"George Watt will..." Sam started to say.

J.J. grabbed Sam's arm. The landscape shimmered in front of their eyes.

A moment later, it stilled.

They were standing in the moonlight on a wooden sidewalk. The caragana hedges were grown high again.

Sam gasped. "We've time travelled again. Geo..."

J.J. clamped her hand over her friend's mouth. "Don't say his name," she hissed. "The last time you said it, he appeared, and this time when you said it, he disappeared."

Sam removed J.J.'s hand. "You think, by just saying Geo..." She felt a poke in the ribs. "Uh, you think if we say his name, we travel through time?"

"It's the only thing I can think of that happened both times we saw him." J.J. held up her hand. "And no, I don't want to try it right now to see if I'm right. We gotta get home."

Whirling on her heels, J.J. started to walk towards the gate, and then halted. "Drat," she muttered, "We're still not in our own time!" She turned back to Sam, her chin sinking to her chest.

"So how do you explain what time we're in right now – whatever it is – and how we got here? We need to figure out what we did, and then maybe we can reverse it." Sam frowned hard in concentration.

"We were standing together on the corner of the foundation. Obviously, we can't do that again with the building sitting on it," J.J. said.

"Did we say anything special?" asked Sam. She twisted her hands as she tried to think.

J.J. scowled up at the two-storey structure. "I don't think so."

"Let's see what else is around here," Sam suggested. "Maybe we'll get an idea."

They walked around the caragana bush and into a huge yard with several buildings. Caragana hedges rimmed the outside edge of the yard like four garrison walls. Over to their right, a small cottage sat near what looked like a huge vegetable garden. The girls could see the silk glisten on the corn cobs in the moonlight, and what looked like rows of hilled potatoes.

"That must be the gardener's cottage Mrs. Goudy mentioned," Sam said.

"And I bet that's the carriage house," J.J. said, pointing to another two-storey building with large barn type doors.

As they started walking around the perimeter of the hedges towards it, the smell of straw and manure wafted on the warm night air. A horse whinnied, and they heard a scuffle of hooves on a wooden floor. A calming voice spoke, and then a figure came through the doorway.

Sam and J.J. ducked into a gap in the hedge and

watched a tall, dark-haired man swing the large wooden door closed. The wooden latch rasped as he slid it into place.

J.J. squirmed closer to Sam. They watched as the man crossed the yard to another small cottage between the carriage house and the staff residence. He held an old-fashioned lantern high to light his way. When he reached the porch, he turned towards the staff residence and held the lantern higher, then swung it slowly from side to side.

"Is he signalling to someone?" J.J. whispered.

Sam wiggled closer to J.J. to get a better look. "Must be."

They fixed their eyes on the building and waited. Less than a minute later, a woman appeared in a top-storey window holding a similar lantern. She waved her hand in front of it, as if sending some kind of code.

"There's his answer," Sam whispered, as the light in the window dimmed, then went out.

The young man extinguished his lantern and set it on the porch step. He stood for a few moments, and then headed towards the residence. When he reached an elm tree surrounded by a clump of bushes, he stopped and waited.

A few moments later, a woman in a summer dress emerged through the door. The man joined her and they clasped hands, and then they hurried towards another corner of the building and out of sight.

"Should we follow them?" Sam asked, already pushing out of the hedge into the open area.

J.J. nodded, and they rushed across the yard. When they reached the building, they kept to the shadows along the outer wall until they reached the corner where the couple had disappeared. They stopped.

"Do you think we should peek around the corner?" Sam glanced back at J.J.

J.J. nodded.

"Ready?" Sam whispered.

"Yes," J.J. whispered back, putting her hand on Sam's shoulder.

Sam placed her hand against the wall.

The girls sprawled to the ground in a heap. The building had vanished.

They lay there gasping for a few moments, and then Sam pushed J.J. off of her. J.J. groaned and rolled onto her back.

"We're back in our own time," Sam sputtered. She sat up and looked at a familiar Dewdney Avenue, with vehicles rushing by blocks of houses with lights on.

"I'm sure glad we are, even if we don't know how we did it," J.J. said.

"I wonder how long we've been gone." Sam sounded worried.

"I don't know, but it's dark, so it's late." J.J. shuddered.

"We'd better get home before our parents come looking for us." Sam jumped up and helped J.J. to her feet. They brushed the leaves off of each other.

"Oh my gosh, there's your backpack. We forgot all about it. I'd be in big trouble if I lost Dad's camera!" Sam found the camera, and J.J. found her flashlight still on.

"Stay clear of that foundation!" J.J. warned. She shone the flashlight along the ground.

"I'm not going anywhere near it," Sam said, taking several steps towards the service road. "I don't like going back in time and not knowing how we did it or if we'll ever get home."

"I don't think I want to come back here ever again." J.J.'s voice still shook. "I don't think I'll get to sleep tonight either."

"What if we hadn't been able to get back?" Sam said with a shiver.

"No one would ever know what happened to us," J.J. croaked.

They walked to the gate, lost in their own thoughts. The night settled down around them, holding them in a cloak of darkness as wind rattled leaves along the roadway. Something was scurrying along with them. Sam pulled her hoodie tighter and stared at the bushes across the grounds, half expecting someone to appear.

Something scuttled in the grass beside them. Sam screamed and bolted. J.J., breathing hard, was right behind her.

CHAPTER FIVE

"WE'RE SURE LUCKY we made it back in time for supper,"
Sam said as she sat on the braided rug in J.J.'s bedroom.
"My folks were already starting to eat." Sam dug into her
backpack and passed J.J. photos of the foundation she'd
taken that afternoon. Her dad had run the photos off for
the girls on his computer.

"We're lucky we made it back at all!" J.J. said. She
plunked herself on a corner of her bed and riffled through
the photos.

"That's for sure." Sam agreed. "But if we *ever were* to
go back there again, these photos would help us find the
foundation."

"I don't want to go there again. That was too scary
going back to two different times like that. Once was
creepy enough." J.J. handed back the photos and lay on
her belly with her hands holding her head. "But I wonder
why it keeps happening?"

"Maybe we're supposed to do something," Sam suggested. "Like last time."

"You mean, how we got all the ghosts to meet each
other, so they weren't lonely?"

Sam nodded.

"But this is different," J.J. said. "This time, we're the ones going back in time. To two different times. So how could they meet each other? And the people we saw weren't even ghosts – they were living in their own time."

"That's true, I guess. Last time, all the ghosts ended up appearing to us at the same time and we could introduce them." Sam tucked her pictures into her backpack.

"At least I can do an accurate drawing of the grounds for my poster, even if no one else will know they're exact."

J.J. laughed. "Yeah, that was really something, to see all those old buildings for real."

"I wouldn't mind going back again," admitted Sam, "to see what they looked like inside and what they were used for."

J.J. glared at her in disbelief.

Sam muttered, "Well, not that I really want to go back, but it *would* be interesting to explore." She wondered how she could talk J.J. into just one more visit.

"I can live without seeing any more," J.J. said firmly. She dropped to the floor beside Sam and pulled her pencil crayons out of her backpack. "We better get our posters finished."

Sam was still looking at J.J. "Are you sure you don't want to see more?"

J.J. looked up in surprise, a flicker of fear in her eyes. "Yes, I'm sure. Don't even think about it any more. I'm not going back!"

"What if it's not on purpose?" asked Sam, secretly hoping that it might happen again by accident.

"We'll make sure we steer clear of the foundation and the basement! And if we remember not to say Geo..." J.J.

stopped short. "*You know who's* name – we'll be fine."

"I hope so," said Sam. "Though we're not entirely sure how we went back and forth in time."

"We know if we say his name, it happens," J.J. said.

"It didn't happen when we asked about him at Mrs. Goudy's," said Sam. "Maybe it only happens when we're on Government House grounds."

"We know enough, and I don't want to test any more theories!" J.J. shoved Sam's poster at her across the floor. "Let's get to work."

Sam giggled. "You sound just like my mom when you get all stern like that."

J.J. put her hands to her hips. "If it makes you stop talking about ghosts or going back in time, I'm fine with sounding like her."

Sam bent over her poster and sketched the diagram of the old grounds at Government House. She blocked in the buildings as best as she could remember. She and J.J. worked in silence, except for the scratching of their pencil crayons. After a while, J.J. switched on her cell phone and turned on some tunes. Sam hummed along to Katy Perry's latest hit.

"I'm done," J.J. said, holding up her poster. She'd drawn and pencil-coloured the clothing styles of the women living in Government House throughout the past 125 years. They were placed sequentially over a faint face of a clock, with the dates of each decade labelled.

"You're so good at art," Sam said. She sat back on her heels. "I'm having trouble with a few things. Do you remember what other buildings there were?"

J.J. thought for a few moments. "It was kind of dark, so I'm not sure. You have the main ones, though."

Sam wrinkled her nose. "Maybe I need to find out more."

J.J. scowled. "No, we're not going back to the foundation."

"I know, I know." Sam held up her hand. "I was thinking about asking Mrs. Goudy instead."

"That would be okay, I guess," J.J. said. "But we'd have to go tomorrow. Our posters are due on Thursday."

"Mrs. Goudy called and left a message with Mom to say I can pick up the pictures tomorrow. How about we go right after school? I'll go home now and get my cell phone and call her to see if that's okay." Sam picked up her drawing gear and stuffed it into her backpack, and then she grabbed her poster, rolled it and placed it in the tube.

"You sure don't waste much time." J.J. laughed. "See you tomorrow morning."

"See ya!" Sam rushed out the door.

❧

J.J. AND SAM crossed Dewdney Avenue and headed towards Pioneer Village. A light autumn breeze flipped strands of their hair, and the late afternoon sun warmed their faces.

"I'm glad Mrs. Goudy agreed to see us again so soon," Sam said.

"It was nice of your mom to bake some gingerbread cookies for us to give her too." J.J. sniffed the cookies as Sam waved the bag in front of her nose.

"I hope she likes them. Mom said it was the least I could do when she's helping me so much with my project."

Sam turned to enter the service gate of Government House, but J.J. pulled her back.

"Let's go down the city sidewalk past the grounds. Then we won't have any problem running into ghosts or slipping back in time."

"It'll take us longer, though," Sam said.

"We'll just walk faster. There's no way I'm going through there, even in the daylight."

J.J. forged ahead with Sam at her heels, the tube with her rolled-up poster smacking against her legs. They made a game of it, hurrying faster and faster, trying to outdo one another, until they were running through the parking lot of the retirement home. Giggling and out of breath, they slipped into the foyer in record time.

Amber welcomed them. "Do you want me to take you to Mrs. Goudy, or do you know the way?"

"We'll be fine on our own, thank you," Sam said. J.J. nodded in agreement as she brushed her hair out of her face.

As soon as they turned into the first long corridor, Sam slowed right down.

"What are you doing?" J.J. asked.

"Hoping Lily, or whoever that woman was, will appear again."

"I hope she doesn't." J.J. glared at Sam, thinking she was just fine without seeing or talking to Lily ever again.

"I'd like to ask her who she is." Sam's eyes twinkled. "Or get you to ask her. She seems to connect with you the most."

J.J. rolled her eyes. "I don't see how that will help us solve the mystery of our time travel. Besides, I'd rather not deal with a ghost right now." She stopped dead in her tacks. "Too late," she whispered.

At the corner stood the woman in the blue flowered dress, observing their approach. She seemed to waver above the floor.

"What?" Sam asked.

"Lily's here."

"Where?"

J.J. leaned closer to Sam and pointed.

"I see her now." Sam nudged J.J. and whispered, "You talk to her."

"Wh-what do I say?" J.J. whispered back.

"Ask her who she is." Sam gave J.J. a little push forward.

"Uh, hello," J.J. said, her heart drumming in her chest.

The ghostly figure continued to look at them with soft, dark blue eyes.

"I'm, uh, I'm Jensyn, uh, J.J., and this is my friend, uh, Samantha."

The apparition didn't speak, but J.J. was sure she glided a few inches closer to them.

The girls stumbled backwards. The translucent woman stood still.

Although her heart pounded in her chest, J.J. found her voice. "Wh-who are you?"

The woman's head tilted, but she didn't say a word.

"Are you Lily?" asked J.J., standing with her hands clutched in front of her.

A brief smile appeared.

"Can we help you, somehow?" Sam asked.

The ghost's face turned sad and finally she mouthed a word. Then she faded into the wall.

J.J. slumped against the wall, clutching her hand to her throat.

Sam sagged beside her.

"Did she just say 'watch'?" J.J. asked.

"That's what I heard too," Sam said.

"What do you think she wants us to watch?" J.J. asked.

"Not a clue," Sam said.

Sam adjusted the poster tube under her arm, and they set off down the hall again, rounding the corner to Mrs. Goudy's suite. Her door was open.

"Come in, girls," she invited. "Please sit down, and tell me about your progress." She patted the arm of the love seat beside her armchair.

Sam presented Mrs. Goudy with the cookies. "These are from my mom."

Mrs. Goudy's eyes lit up as she opened the lid of the plastic container. "Gingerbread cookies. How thoughtful. Thank you." She held out the container to the girls.

J.J. and Sam each selected a cookie and sat on the love seat. Mrs. Goudy chose one and set the container on the table between them.

"Mmm. Home-made, freshly baked. Divine," Mrs. Goudy said, biting into one with a rapturous smile. "This takes me back to when I worked at Government House during the Christmas holidays. All the baking we did to distribute to the less fortunate and for the New Year's levee." Her eyes glistened, as she remembered the past. She looked at the girls again with a puzzled expression, but shook it off.

"Sounds like a busy time," Sam said.

"Oh yes, but so much fun getting everything prepared and decorated and seeing all the delighted smiles of people coming to visit." She brought herself back to the present. "My goodness, dears, you'll need something to drink. Please help yourselves to refreshments from the fridge."

"May I get you something too?" J.J. asked on her way to the kitchen, with Sam trailing behind her.

"A little apple juice, please. The glasses are in the cupboard to the right of the sink."

When the girls returned, Mrs. Goudy handed Sam an envelope. "Your photographs. I hope they'll be useful to you."

J.J. leaned over Sam's shoulder as she looked through them. "These are perfect. Thank you!" Sam pulled some money out of her jacket pocket. "How much do I owe you for them?"

"Oh nothing, dear," said Mrs. Goudy, pushing Sam's outstretched hand back. "Amber took photographs of all the old photos and printed them on paper in the office, so it didn't cost me anything."

"That's very kind of you," Sam said, flushing. "I really didn't expect you to do this for nothing."

"I know, but I wanted to do it. I enjoy your company. Now what else have you to show me?" Mrs. Goudy leaned forward as Sam tugged her poster out of the tube.

J.J. moved a few items and helped Sam spread it on the coffee table in front of them.

"You've done remarkably well from what I told you," said Mrs. Goudy, her eyes widening in surprise. "It's almost as if you'd seen the grounds yourself."

J.J. glanced sideways at Sam, who shot her a little grin.

"You gave me good information," Sam said. She pulled a pencil out of her pocket.

"You certainly took good notes," Mrs. Goudy said. "I

didn't think I'd given you so much detail."

Sam stuttered. "I guess it's because you made it sound so real." She stared down at the poster. "I'm sure I missed some things, though."

Sam looked up again at Mrs. Goudy. "I wonder if you could tell me what some of these other buildings are or if I have them in the right place."

As they studied Sam's drawing, Mrs. Goudy filled in where the well, the pump house, and the vegetable garden were located, and named some of the smaller buildings. She pointed out Bert's house again.

"He's the one who took out your sister Lily for a while, right?" J.J. asked. She reached for her cookie and took another bite.

"Yes, they spent a great deal of time together that one summer."

Suddenly, J.J. nudged Sam's arm and pointed. Lily stood on the other side of the room in her blue flowered dress, staring at them.

Sam choked on a piece of cookie and began coughing. J.J. thumped her back and handed her a glass of juice.

Mrs. Goudy looked at her in alarm.

"I'm okay," said Sam, recovering. "I guess some crumbs got caught in my throat."

"As long as you're all right."

"Yes, I am, thank you. Though I will get a glass of water, if that's okay."

"Certainly, dear." Mrs. Goudy smoothed her hair and looked at Sam's poster again.

"I'd like some too." J.J. led the way to the kitchen, with Sam on her heels. "Would you like us to get you more apple juice, Mrs. Goudy?"

"I'm fine for now."

J.J. kept her eye on the ghostly figure of Lily as they crossed the room. As soon as they were out of sight, J.J. grabbed Sam's arm and whispered, "What should we do about Lily?"

"Should we ask Mrs. Goudy if she can see her?" Sam asked. She turned on the water tap and let the water get cold.

J.J. shrugged. "We don't want to frighten her," she whispered.

"Maybe the ghost will just go away and we won't have to say anything," Sam whispered back. She rinsed out her juice glass and filled it with water.

"Finding everything all right?" called Mrs. Goudy.

"Yes, thank you," J.J. called from the kitchen. Sam turned off the tap and they started back into the living room.

J.J. glanced quickly across the room. Lily was still there, her dark curly hair in a short bob, her head tilted, staring at them. J.J. hurried to sit tight beside Sam again on the love seat.

J.J. faced Mrs. Goudy, her eyes averted from Lily's direction. "So what would a young couple do in the evening, if they went out together back when you worked there?"

"Usually go for a walk, or to a local café for coffee, or for an ice cream cone in the summer. There was one little shop down the street quite a ways, but going there made for a nice evening jaunt, especially if the weather was decent. Or, as I mentioned before, we'd go to the movies on Saturday night once a month." Mrs. Goudy shifted in her chair. "There wasn't much money around in those days. We didn't have a car or money to spend on gasoline. We had to walk or take a street car. On a special occasion, we might go to a dance."

"What about if you wanted to spend some time together, but not leave the property?" asked Sam.

"There were some lovely little walkways through the grounds, and a few benches to sit on. If you wanted to get cozy with a fella, there was a nice little alcove of trees that offered some privacy for a serious chat," Mrs. Goudy said with a faraway look.

"Did you go there with anyone special?" J.J. asked timidly.

"Not really." Suddenly Mrs. Goudy sat up straighter. She gave a fleeting glance toward the photograph of the young man J.J. had noticed on her previous visit. Then she busied herself placing the lid on the cookie container.

"I didn't go in for that kind of stuff as much as my older sister, Lily. She sure enjoyed Bert's company. I'd never seen her so happy." Mrs. Goudy's face lit up at the memory. "I thought they could have been happy together, but then that movie star came along. Bert started taking on airs and ignoring Lily until she turned away."

J.J. ventured a look at Lily. She looked sad.

For a few moments, Mrs. Goudy sat in thought. "When Bert decided he wanted her back, it was too late. She'd already met her husband. I always wondered if she regretted her decision."

J.J. walked over to the wall of photos and stared at the one of Mrs. Goudy and her sister. She glanced back at the figure across the room. No doubt about it, she was the same person as in the photograph.

"Didn't you say your sister died young, not long after

this photograph was taken?" J.J. asked, returning to sit beside Sam. "You don't have to tell us why," she added in a rush. "It's not really any of our business."

"I'm fine telling you. It's so long ago now, it's not as painful as it once was to talk about." Mrs. Goudy spoke softly. "She died during the influenza epidemic of 1943. She was the picture of health when she went with her husband to Alberta to visit his family. She became too ill to even come back. She returned in a pine box and was buried in her husband's family plot at Ogema."

Mrs. Goudy looked as sad as Lily.

J.J. wiggled to the edge of the love seat, to be close to Mrs. Goudy. She patted her hand. "I'm sorry I brought back sad memories. She looks like she was lots of fun." J.J. suddenly thought of her own mother, and how much fun they used to have together before she had died.

Mrs. Goudy rubbed J.J.'s hand. "Yes, we had great times together." Mrs. Goudy laughed. "You wouldn't believe the mischief we got into when we were young."

J.J. glanced across the room. Lily was smiling. J.J. turned back to Mrs. Goudy. "She's sure pretty in that blue flowered dress she's wearing in the photo," she said, hoping to lighten the mood.

"Yes, that was her favourite dress. A birthday gift from Bert."

Suddenly, Mrs. Goudy stopped and stared at J.J. "How do you know it was blue flowered? The photo is in black-and-white."

J.J. froze.

"Didn't you mention it last time?" J.J. asked. She stared at the woman across the room, then at Sam, and then back at Mrs. Goudy.

"I don't recall telling you that," said Mrs. Goudy with a puzzled expression.

"Lucky guess," J.J. suggested, twisting a piece of her hair in her fingers.

Mrs. Goudy tilted her head and stared at J.J. and Sam. "I don't think that's it," she said.

She clasped her hands and gazed at them for several moments. When she looked away, her eyes went immediately across the room, towards Lily. "You see her too, don't you?"

J.J. felt a long shiver trickle up her back, from the base of her spine to the top of her neck. Beside her, Sam gasped.

CHAPTER SIX

SAM RECOVERED FIRST. "What did you say?"

"You can see Lily too. *That's* how you know what colour of dress she's wearing." Mrs. Goudy's voice had dropped lower.

Sam and J.J. nodded.

"Does she speak to you?" J.J. asked.

Mrs. Goudy shook her head. "No, but I know she wants to tell me something. We can't seem to communicate."

"How long have you been able to see her?"

"Not until you girls showed up the first time," Mrs. Goudy said. "Oh, I felt her presence around me before and was comforted by that, but I'd never actually seen her." She winked at her sister. "It's so lovely to see you again after all this time. I've missed you so."

Lily's ghostly face lit up with a broad smile.

"Lily, is there something we need to know?" J.J. asked in a soft voice.

The young woman's face went solemn. She looked like she was trying to form a response.

"Can we do anything for you?" Sam croaked, excited to have a puzzle to solve.

"Watch," she seemed to mouth again. Then her

apparition faded away.

"That's what she told us before," J.J. said, putting her hands on her hips.

"You've seen her before?" Mrs. Goudy asked.

"Yes," J.J. said.

"The first time we visited you," Sam said.

"Where was that, girls?" Mrs. Goudy sat up straighter and turned towards them.

"She was in the hall. We thought it was you coming to meet us," J.J explained.

"I don't get around as easily anymore," Mrs. Goudy said. "So I wouldn't have come to meet you, but that is certainly a curious incident."

Sam and J.J. nodded.

Mrs. Goudy furrowed her eyebrows in thought. "But I wonder what we're supposed to watch."

"We haven't come up with any ideas so far." Sam leaned forward, thinking hard about the puzzle again.

"She seems to think *we* should know, though," J.J. said.

"Or that we should be able to figure it out," Sam added.

Mrs. Goudy shook her head. "I don't know what she could possibly want us to watch."

"Is something coming up that could be important to both of you?" J.J. asked.

"Like a special birthday, or an anniversary, maybe?" Sam said.

Mrs. Goudy shrugged. "I can't think what it could be."

"What about something from your past?" J.J. asked.

"Not that I know of." Mrs. Goudy seemed stumped. "Especially if it involves you two as well. It's a mystery to me."

Suddenly, the pendulum clock on the wall chimed five

times.

Everyone looked at it at once. Sam sensed that the chimes marked some kind of urgency for them to solve the mystery before time ran out.

"We're going to have to head home," Sam said.

"My supper time too." Mrs. Goudy turned back to them and grinned.

"Will you be all right on your own, if we leave you now, Mrs. Goudy?" J.J. asked.

"Oh yes, girls. I'm fine." She looked amused. "I'm not the least bit scared, if that's what you're worried about."

"The thought crossed my mind," Sam admitted, feeling just a bit rattled herself.

"It is a little strange, but after all, it's only my dear sister," Mrs. Goudy said. "I'm thrilled to see her again."

"We'll just tidy up a bit before we go," J.J. said. She took the juice and water glasses to the kitchen.

"Thank you. You girls are such a delight," Mrs. Goudy said. "Don't worry about doing the dishes. I'll have plenty of time later."

Sam brought a cloth from the kitchen and wiped the table where they'd had their snack. "Shall I leave the cookies here within reach?" she asked. "Or would you like me to put them in the kitchen?"

"The kitchen, please. Just on the counter is fine. I've already spoiled my supper a little," Mrs. Goudy patted her stomach, "but it was well worth it. Please thank your mom for me."

"I will," Sam said, as she rolled her poster and slipped it back into the protective tube. "And thank you for all of your help. And for the photographs!"

"You'll come back for another visit, won't you?" Mrs.

Goudy looked sad that she might not see them again.

"You bet we will," J.J. said. "We'll help you figure out what Lily wants, if you'd like us to."

"I'd enjoy that," Mrs. Goudy said. "And I want to know how you make out with that poster contest too. Don't make it too long before your next visit."

"We won't," Sam said.

Mrs. Goudy reached out to each of the girls for a hand and clasped them in hers. "See you soon," she said, as they took their leave.

Sam thanked Amber at the reception desk for her help with the photos, but Sam was so deep in thought that she didn't say a word to J.J. until they were at the foyer door. The light had faded, and mounds of grey clouds had built up in the darkening skies.

"Oh no. It's going to rain," J.J. said.

"It'll be faster if we cut through the grounds of Government House," Sam said.

J.J. shook her head. "I don't want to go that way. I've had enough of ghosts for now."

A smattering of rain landed on their heads.

"We'll be soaked if we don't. We'll run; it won't take long," Sam said.

"Only if we stick to the lighted paths," J.J. warned. "And we don't go anywhere near the places where we've gone back into the past."

"Agreed! Let's go!" Sam took off like a shot. J.J. overtook her at the first bend in the walkway.

Light rain fell through the bare branches of the trees. They ran on, holding their hoodies tight, Sam awkwardly clutching her poster tube under her arm.

As the rain came down harder, J.J. shrieked. "Faster!"

Sam turned her face towards the sky. The rain pelted her face, and its surprising warmth felt good, though her vision was blurred from the moisture pouring down her forehead. She ducked her head, shook off the rain and pressed onward.

All at once, her left foot slipped off the wet, paved blocks. Sam sprawled onto the ground into a clump of soggy leaves.

"Wait, J.J.," she called, as she picked herself up.

J.J. ran back to help her.

"Darn, I've messed up my best jeans." Sam wiped the mucky mess of leaves and mud off of her knees.

"Isn't this like a déjà vu thing, with us sprawling on the ground?" J.J. said, handing Sam a tissue from her pocket.

"We do seem to be picking ourselves up off the ground a lot lately," Sam said, rubbing her hands with the tissue. "Ever since we ran into George Watt."

"No!" shouted J.J., too late to clamp her hand over Sam's mouth.

Abruptly, the scene changed.

J.J. GROANED BESIDE Sam under a late afternoon sun. She gaped across the stark grounds to the main house. George trundled away from the rose garden with his wheelbarrow, empty this time except for a rake laid on an angle across the top.

"I'm so sorry," Sam moaned.

"Me too," J.J. grumbled next to her. "We didn't need this right now!" Why was Sam always getting them into trouble?

Sam had a sudden idea. "But now that we're here, maybe we can find out more about why we keep seeing Geo…, and maybe it will stop happening."

"Maybe," J.J. said. She really didn't want to face anything more right now.

Sam was already limping towards George.

"Are you okay to walk?" J.J. asked, catching up. She removed her wet hoodie and tucked it over her arm.

"Just twisted my knee a little. I'll be fine," Sam said. She rubbed it, tied her hoodie around her waist, and continued on.

Just then, George caught sight of them. He set the wheelbarrow down and waved. As he waited for them, he pulled his chain from his vest pocket. He looked surprised when there was nothing on the end of it. He examined his vest pocket again and patted down his pant pockets. Scratching his head, he searched the ground, and then glanced at the sun. It was perched low in the sky, above the open prairie.

"Good afternoon, young ladies," he said, when they were closer. His face still held a puzzled look. "Although I seem to have misplaced my watch. I believe it's time to call it a day outside and check the progress of the mushrooms. Perhaps you'd like to come with me?" he invited.

"Mushroom watching, just what we need," mumbled Sam under her breath.

"You're the one who got us into this," J.J. reminded her friend in a whisper. Out loud to George, she tried to be enthusiastic. "Sounds great."

George rattled the wheelbarrow over to a small shed, upended it against the wall, and then perched his rake upright next to it.

"We'll just take a peek, and then see if we can get back home again," Sam said.

"It should be easy enough, seeing as how we only seem to have to say his name," J.J. said. "In fact, we could say it right now."

"No, wait!" Sam said. "We might as well take a quick look while we're here."

"Fine," J.J. said, crossing her arms sternly. "But we're not hanging around for long."

Sam agreed. J.J. shuffled along beside her, hands in her jacket pockets. Why did she always wind up agreeing with Sam? She supposed it was because a small part of her was curious too.

They followed George into the basement through the back door, down the dimly-lit hallway and into the warm, moist room lined with wooden beds. When her eyes adjusted, J.J. saw a mass of small white polkadots, like marshmallows of various sizes, nudging out of the soil.

George stood with a pleased smile. Then he picked up a basket.

"They're best when they are still small like these," he said. "You gently rotate them." With a gentle turn of his wrist, he demonstrated how to pick the tender morsels.

"You try," George said. "Just pick one at a time."

Sam and J.J. each reached for one.

"This is easy," J.J. said. She bent to pick several more, careful not to touch any other mushrooms next to the one she plucked.

As they worked, the hissing of the steam system surrounded them. J.J. brushed her moist hair from her face and continued on, feeling satisfied as the basket filled.

"You can eat them raw too," George said. He rubbed

the flecks of dirt off of one. His face lit up as he popped it into his mouth.

J.J. followed his example. "Mmm. More flavour than those you buy. I've never had one this fresh before."

George cleaned one and handed it to Sam. She took a cautious nibble as the others watched.

"Not bad," she said, and popped the rest into her mouth.

Once they'd filled the basket, George allowed them to step into the hallway first, and then closed the door securely.

"With any luck, you can have some for your next meal," George said. "I need to go back to the rose garden to look for my watch. But first, let's take these up to the kitchen to be cleaned."

J.J. and Sam looked at one another. An unspoken question passed between them: Should they go with him or leave for home?

Sam shook her head and whispered. "We can't let anyone else see us."

J.J. nodded her head towards the back door. She wanted to leave *right now*. There was no way she wanted to have any more encounters or do more exploring.

"Uh, we're supposed to be somewhere else right now," Sam said, but George was already part way down the hall.

"We won't be able to come with you," called J.J. after him, but he did not hear them, nor realize they weren't following. They needed to get his attention.

"Mr. Watt," Sam called after him. At the same time, J.J. yelled, "Uh, George."

Within a blink of an eye, the girls were standing under a moonlit sky, in the yard overgrown with caraganas.

"Sheesh!" said Sam. She whirled around. "We never even got to say goodbye to him. He'll think we're rude."

"What's worse is that we didn't go back to our own time," J.J. said, looking at the thousands of stars winking overhead in the warm summer night.

"Maybe we're back with Bert and Lily?" Sam said.

"Hard to tell," J.J. said. She gazed across the landscape studded with various buildings and the inevitable grid of caraganas.

They moved along the wall of the staff quarters, passed an herb garden and went on towards the wooden sidewalk that led to the back door of the main house.

"At least it's not raining." Sam shivered.

"Small help." J.J. scowled at Sam. "What do we do now?"

"Let's head to the staff residence," J.J. said, tugging at Sam's hand. "Maybe we can go to the same corner and find our way back from there."

"I don't think so," Sam said, staring across the yard. "At least not until we figure out what's happening over there."

J.J. stopped and gaped at the fancy carriage pulled by four horses, clopping through the main entrance towards Government House. Two drivers in dark uniforms and white hats sat high up in the front seats, white-gloved hands holding the jangling reins.

"It's the landau that was on display in the foyer!" Sam said, breathless with wonder. "I wonder who's in it." The carriage proceeded along the drive and disappeared around the front of the mansion.

"His Honour and Mrs. McNab with..." said a voice behind them.

J.J. screamed and raced away. In a minute, she realized she couldn't hear Sam's footsteps pounding behind her.

CHAPTER SEVEN

"OH, I SAY, I didn't mean to startle you."

Sam whirled to face an older man with dark hair, neatly trimmed, standing before her in a black suit and vest, with a white shirt and black bow tie. His hazel eyes looked concerned.

"Who are you?" Sam demanded. Her heart pounded so loud, she thought he could hear it. So loud, she couldn't hear J.J. running any more either. What had happened to her? She darted a glance over her shoulder, but J.J. wasn't there. Sam swallowed hard. She turned back to the man.

"Ernie Myles, miss. I'm the outside gardener, doubling as the butler tonight." He offered her his gloved hand. "Excuse the gloves. They're a beast to get on and off, and I'll need them on again in a moment."

Sam shook his hand with the tips of her fingers.

"Sam, get away from him," J.J. yelled from across the grounds.

"It's okay, J.J.," called Sam. "This is Ernie Myles."

J.J. trotted up to them and stared at Ernie.

"Hello, miss," he said, his eyes crinkled at the corners as he nodded at J.J.

Suddenly, the back door of the house opened, and a

young woman in a black dress and a large, draping white collar with a bib-like apron poked her head out.

She called cheerily, "There you are, Ernie. The guests are arriving."

"Coming," he said.

J.J. stared wide-eyed at the woman. "Isn't...isn't that Lily," she stuttered.

"Sure looks like it," Sam said. A shiver ran up the back of her neck.

"You're right." Ernie looked at J.J. in surprise.

"Oh, I see there's someone else there." Lily stepped onto the back step. "Who are you chatting with?"

"I'm not rightly sure," he said, turning back to look at the girls.

Lily closed the back door and walked towards them. Her sensible black shoes tapped on the wooden sidewalk.

"A couple of young waifs by the looks of them." Ernie gave them a quick smile. "They seem to know who you are."

J.J. shrunk back a little. Sam stood rooted to the spot.

"I don't believe we've met," Lily said as she joined them.

Sam was sure Lily couldn't possibly know who they were. At least not when she had been living at Government House, like she was doing right now.

"We actually haven't met," Sam said. Not in the normal sense of meeting people, anyway. She wasn't sure if ghosts counted.

J.J. came to the rescue. "Someone showed us a photograph with you in it."

"You recognized me from a photo? That's really good." She laughed. Then she turned serious. "But what on earth are you doing out here? Where's your family?"

Before Sam could answer, the back door was flung open again.

"Lily, Ernie. Hurry!" A blonde-haired woman in a similar outfit to Lily waved them in.

"Coming, Alice," Lily's voice sang out.

Sam realized with a start that Alice was Mrs. Goudy when she was a young housekeeper. How pretty she looked.

As Lily swivelled to return to the house, she called over her shoulder. "Do you need help finding your way?"

"We're fine," Sam said. "Our family is just over there." She pointed vaguely towards the avenue.

"We were just watching the landau arrive," J.J. said.

Ernie touched his forehead. "We'll be seeing you then." He hurried after Lily.

Sam felt her pulse drop, as Lily and Ernie made it inside and the door closed behind them.

"We got to see Lily and Alice when they worked here," J.J. said. She exhaled in a long whistle.

"Lily seems really nice," Sam said. "I wish we could see more."

"Oh no you don't," J.J. said. "We're in enough trouble now. We've got to get home." J.J. stomped off without looking back.

Sam ignored J.J. "I'm just going to take a little peek," she said to herself.

She tiptoed up the sidewalk and tried the doorknob. It turned. Slowly, she eased the door open a crack. Wonderful smells of roast duck and simmering vegetables and sauces wafted out. There was no one in the entryway. Opening the door wider, she slipped inside and crossed the vestibule to the edge of the kitchen.

Steam rose from several large pots cooking on a huge range, their lids plop-plopping rhythmically. A woman with dark hair coiled on top of her head stirred each pot in turn, then moved to a long table in the centre of the room. She arranged canapés on several platters on the table. Beneath her feet, the floor was covered with the decorative ceramic tiles Mrs. Goudy had told them about. Sam's lips curved with pleasure.

Next to the cook, Ernie opened bottles of wine and set them on a gleaming silver serving tray. "The guests are in high spirits tonight," he said. "And it looks like you've outdone yourself to match the occasion, Kate."

"It is rather special to have Princess Alice and the Earl of Athlone here for dinner again," Kate said.

"Yes, it's not everyone who gets a visit from the Governor General of Canada, nor twice in one year," Ernie replied.

"And only five months ago." Kate threw him a look of exasperation.

"A lot of work for you, but they sure enjoyed your meal in April," Ernie said. "Said you were a superb cook."

"Thank you," Kate said, looking pleased.

With practiced ease, Ernie balanced the wine salver on his shoulder and proceeded towards the dining room.

Sam leaned forward, trying to look through the kitchen at the guests in the dining room, but Kate glanced her way. Sam ducked back into the vestibule. Her heart gave a lurch. She had to be more careful.

The next time she dared peek around the door frame was when she heard someone else enter the kitchen. Instantly, she drew back and listened. Two women were talking. Sam poked her head out again. Alice and Lily stood by the table in the centre of the kitchen that held the canapés.

"You came in rather late last night," Alice said, glancing at Lily with a little smile. "With preparing all day, I haven't even had a chance to ask you how Bert liked his birthday gift."

Lily beamed. "He said he liked it just fine. The best thing anyone has ever given him." Lily paused. "But..."

"But what?" Alice looked at Lily.

Sam pressed herself closer to the door frame to see and hear better.

"It's nothing really. I just wonder if he was really pleased, or just said he was." A flicker of doubt crossed Lily's face.

"You silly goose. Of course, he was pleased. You need to get over worrying about how you came to get the pocket watch for him." Alice eyed the trays.

"You don't think I should tell him I found it on the grounds?" Lily tugged her apron straighter.

"Why on earth would you do that?" Alice shook her head. "All he needs to know is that you cared enough to get one for him. He'll figure you spotted it in a second-hand store. Where else would you get a lovely antique like that?" Alice patted Lily on the back. "He'd have done the same. None of us can afford to buy antiques from a special collector, or anything of that quality brand new. It's become rather a fun and expected thing to find such second-hand treasurers where we can."

"Well, if you're sure."

"Of course, I'm sure. It's a very special gift, and he's lucky you had it refurbished too."

Lily's face brightened again. "It did turn out rather well."

A little bell tinkled on the wall next to the dining room door.

Alice gave Lily a grin and hoisted a tray over her shoulder. "Time to serve the canapés." She sailed out of the kitchen. Lily whisked another tray up and followed her sister out.

Sam eased back into the entryway. There was no way she'd be able to get past Kate to see into the dining room. And J.J. was probably frantically worrying about her. The tea kettle whistled as Sam tiptoed back across the vestibule and to the back door.

She'd barely closed the outside door, when a hand grabbed her arm. Sam jumped and stumbled backwards.

❦

"WHAT WERE YOU doing?" demanded J.J. "You left me out here on my own."

"You didn't want to come," Sam grumbled. "Besides, I wasn't gone long."

"Long enough! It's creepy out here all alone." J.J. blinked back tears and swallowed hard to calm her anger.

A guilty look flashed across Sam's face. "Sorry! I won't do it again. I promise, J. J. At least, not on purpose."

"Not at any time. From now on we stick close together, no matter what happens."

"Agreed," Sam said.

"I want to go home *now*." J.J. grabbed Sam's arm and pulled her across the shadowy grounds. "Will it work if we touch the staff building?"

"I hope so," Sam said.

Halfway across the grounds, Sam slowed. "Sorry, my knee is bugging me," she said, bending to rub it.

"Doesn't look like we're going to get back home so fast anyway," J.J. said. "Look over there."

"Oh no," Sam said.

Two men stood close together on the path to the staff residence. Right where they needed to be.

"I thought everyone was helping inside the main house," J.J. said.

"Must be the coachmen of the landau."

"Isn't one of them Bert?" J.J. asked.

"I think you're right."

J.J. looked around. Was there another way to get past them? "We could go the long way around the staff residence, I guess."

"That'll take too long in the dark. I wonder if we could distract them somehow."

"I don't see any rocks to throw," J.J. said.

"Let's get closer to see what they're talking about," Sam suggested. "Maybe we can figure out what their plans are."

J.J. and Sam edged nearer, keeping to the shadows of trees and bushes, being careful about where they stepped.

"Slow down," Sam hissed. She bent down and rubbed her knee.

"Are you going to be okay?" J.J. asked quietly. "Maybe we need to come up with another plan." She wasn't sure what they'd be able to do if Sam couldn't run.

"I'll be fine," Sam whispered. "I just needed a break."

"We're not close enough yet," J.J. said. The men's voices were louder now, but she still couldn't hear what they were saying. J.J. pointed to a caragana hedge. "Can you make it that far?"

Sam nodded. J.J. dashed toward the hedge, with Sam limping behind her. They burrowed into it.

One of the men laughed. Bert showed the other man something that glinted in the moonlight.

"You're one lucky devil, Bert, to have a swell gal like Lily give you such a great pocket watch," said the second man.

"Don't I know it," he said.

"The carving on it means it was expensive."

"Yes, she's a thing of beauty. All I need now is a silver chain." Bert polished the watch with a handkerchief while J.J. peered through the caragana branches for a better look.

"That should be easy enough to find in a second-hand shop."

"That's where Lily probably got such a fine watch in the first place," Bert said. "I've always wanted a pocket watch, just like my granddad had. It's a similar age to his old time piece." Bert looked at his watch with pride. "Quite exquisite. I'm ever so grateful to her."

"What happened to the family watch?"

"My pops gave it to my older brother." Bert scowled. "Said it was his by rights."

"I suppose it was," said the other man. "Things like that pass down to the oldest in the family."

"Only thing is, my brother didn't care about it at all. But he wouldn't give it to me."

"Then you made out fine with this one." The other man slapped him on the back. "Is it time we got back to the horses and got them rigged up for the drive back with the first guests?"

Bert flicked open the cover of the watch and angled the face towards the moonlight. "No, we have some time yet." He laughed and slipped his watch into his pocket. "You're just anxious to get back to the barracks for some *shut-eye*, Constable Roup," he teased the other man.

"Won't deny it," Roup said. "I like these assignments, but not the waiting around part in between. I'd rather be doing much more serious RCMP work. I like to keep busy."

"I know what you mean," Bert said, as they took a couple of steps away.

J.J. saw, with some relief, that the men strolled across the yard, chatting. But they didn't go far before they settled against a clump of trees, to wait.

"Did you see that watch?" J.J. eased herself onto her knees.

"Yes, a shiny silver one." Sam squatted beside her.

"Now what?" J.J. asked. The men were still too close to them. "We can't stay here until they leave. We're really late now." J.J. had no idea how the time was changing in the present. For how long had they actually been gone?

"What if we made a run for it?" Sam asked. "They might see us, but before they could stop us we might be gone. If my guess is right, I think our time travel has something to do with the corner of the house."

J.J. agreed, "At least every time we're here together, it's happened that way. And we've been touching each other too, so that probably has something to do with it."

"I'm sure we have to touch each other *and* the corner of the building at the same time. Otherwise one of us might get left behind," added Sam.

"We'll have to hold hands tight and not let go." J.J.'s heart thumped. She stared at Sam. "You can run okay with your knee?"

"I'll be fine." Sam hesitated. "It might not work. We might be stuck here." Her voice trembled.

Biting her lip, J.J. said. "But we've got to try."

Sam nodded. "First, we've got to get past this hedge."

J.J. lay on her stomach and wormed along the bottom of the hedge, pulling herself forward with her elbows. She could hear Sam scuffing behind her. The men's voices and bouts of laughter floated towards them, and an occasional waft of wind rustled the leaves. Otherwise, all was quiet on the night air as they crawled along the bushes.

When J.J. reached the end of the caragana hedge farthest from the men, she stood up in the shadows. Sam stood up beside her. They had to cross the boardwalk to get to the corner of the house; there was no other way.

J.J. looked towards the men, and then at Sam. "Does it matter which one of us touches the corner first? You've always been the one to do it."

"I don't know," Sam said.

"You touch it first, just in case," J.J. said.

"Okay." Sam clamped J.J.'s hand in hers. "You ready?"

J.J. squeezed tighter. "Ready."

"Okay. On the count of three."

J.J. took a deep breath. "One, two, THREE!" She shot off with Sam's fingers clasped tight in hers.

They dashed across the last few feet of ground together, clattered over the wooden walk, and dived towards the building, past a small bush. J.J.'s clothing snagged on a bramble, but she tugged it loose.

"Hey, who's there?" one of the men yelled. They heard

pounding feet.

J.J. and Sam scrambled for the corner, hanging tight onto each other's hands.

Sam reached for the corner first. J.J. bumped into her. She saw Sam's hand slip, then Sam reached again. Connected.

The building disappeared.

J.J. fell to the ground, rolling, landing next to Sam. They were on their backs, and the rain fell gently on their faces.

J.J. giggled, happy to be back in their time. She stopped instantly. This really wasn't funny. They could have been stuck in the past forever. She wiped the rain off her face, or was it tears?

She glanced over at Sam.

"We made it, Sam." J.J.'s whole body shook.

Sam heaved a long sigh.

J.J. jumped up and used her sleeve to wipe her face. Beside her, Sam rose to her feet. They looked at the familiar scene of their present time. And there, on the driveway, was Sam's poster tube.

J.J. picked it up and handed it to Sam.

"The tube is wet, but it's still solid. Maybe the poster will be okay." Sam tucked into under her arm. "I've got to finish it right away."

J.J. linked her arm tightly into Sam's. "Let's get home."

CHAPTER EIGHT

With a cup of hot chocolate warming her insides, Sam snuggled into bed, pulling the covers up to her chin. Her mind whirred, though. Maybe she should phone J.J. to discuss their night. She had to tell her friend what she'd heard in the kitchen between Lily and Alice about the watch. But suddenly, Sam felt sleepy.

Before she knew it, J.J. was at her side, shaking her. "Come on, Sam. We're going to be late for school. You slept in."

Sam groaned. "I forgot to set my alarm last night. My parents had to leave early this morning." She opened an eye to peer at her friend. J.J. had dark circles under her eyes.

"Are you okay?" Sam opened both eyes and sat up for a better look. "You look terrible."

"I didn't sleep much," J.J. said. "I had nightmares all night."

"Maybe you should stay home from school," Sam suggested.

J.J. shook her head. "No, I'll be fine. Besides, I want to hand in my poster today."

Sam groaned. She still needed to paste the photographs

on hers.

"How's your poster?" J.J. asked. "Was it dry?"

"It's okay, considering our adventures last night. But I'll have to stay in at lunchtime or after school to get it done."

"Good. That means no more exploring the past." J.J. looked relieved.

"Except..."

"Except nothing," J.J. said. "There's no reason to do any more."

Sam shrugged. "I was just going to say, except I wouldn't mind going to see Mrs. Goudy one more time. I want to ask her about a watch."

"A watch?"

"Wait until I tell you what I overheard last night."

J.J. groaned. "Get dressed while you're telling me. We've gotta get going."

As Sam raced around throwing on her clothes and grabbing her poster and backpack, she told J.J. about the watch Lily had given Bert.

"I bet it's the same one *you know who* lost." Sam couldn't contain her excitement.

"That's a leap," J.J. said, shaking her head.

"Might not be," Sam said. "Think about what Lily's ghost said. The word, 'watch.' I don't think she wants us to watch anything. I think she's trying to tell us something about the watch."

J.J. pursed her lips. "You might be right."

"We just need to find out."

"Oh no, we're not going back there again," J.J. said shrilly. Crossing her arms tightly, she took a step back from Sam.

"No, I mean, we just need to ask Mrs. Goudy what she knows about the watch Lily found. Where and when she found it."

J.J. relaxed. "That's okay then. We can do that."

"Maybe we can even ask Lily herself." Sam grinned.

J.J. laughed. "You really are crazy about connecting with ghosts."

"I thought you were too." Sam looked at J.J. in surprise.

"I was, until this scary going-back-in-time stuff started happening." J.J. clenched her hands together.

"Yeah, wasn't expecting that." Sam raised her eyebrows. "But it sure has been interesting, hasn't it?"

"You could say that." J.J. headed to the door. Sam snapped off her light and they left the room.

By the end of the school day, J.J. looked even more dragged-out. Sam felt sorry for her friend shuffling along beside her.

"Are you sure you're not too tired to come with me to Mrs. Goudy's?" she asked.

"We won't be more than a few minutes, right?"

"No. Mrs. Goudy doesn't have much time for us today, anyway. When I phoned at noon, she said she has an event to go to."

"Then I'll come, but no messing around afterwards."

"Straight there, straight home. City sidewalk all the way. Broad daylight," Sam promised.

J.J. straightened her backpack. "I'm ready, then."

As they set off, they reviewed their adventures of the night before. By the time they reached the Pioneer Village parking lot, they were laughing.

"Can you imagine how shocked Bert and the other guy

must have been when we disappeared before their eyes?" Sam doubled over in a fit of giggles.

J.J. snickered. "I wonder how they tried to explain it. Or if anyone would believe them?"

"Maybe they didn't dare tell anyone." Sam opened the foyer door, and they stepped inside.

"You girls are sure cheerful today," Amber greeted them. "Mrs. Goudy's waiting for you." She waved them by.

Sam felt a little disappointed that they didn't meet Lily in the hallway, even though they walked slowly. Maybe she'd be with Mrs. Goudy?

Mrs. Goudy turned a broad smile on them when they reached her open doorway. "Come in, tell me your news. You sounded so excited on the phone."

Sam and J.J. slid their backpacks to the floor by the door and scuttled to the love seat beside Mrs. Goudy, her eyes sparkling in anticipation.

She eyed J.J. "I don't like to say anything, but are you getting enough rest, dear? Not working too hard on these posters?"

"Uh, just didn't sleep so well last night," J.J. answered, stifling a yawn.

"Maybe too excited about your news? So tell me what you discovered." She settled her hands in her lap and gave them her full attention.

"It's not really news, but more of an idea. It involves your sister Lily and what she said to us," Sam said, peering at Mrs. Goudy.

Mrs. Goudy nodded, her eyes curious.

"Remember she said the word 'watch'?" J.J said.

Mrs. Goudy nodded again.

"We think she meant us to look for a watch, not watch for something." Sam leaned forward.

"There just didn't seem to be anything for us to watch for. I mean, we're working on these posters, and mine is from around the time you worked there with all the staff and the buildings, but, well, we just wondered, that's all." Sam dwindled off and sank back into the love seat. J.J. rustled beside her, looking uncomfortable.

"Do you recall anything about a watch?" J.J. asked.

Mrs. Goudy thought for a moment. "A watch doesn't mean anything to me." She shook her head.

"What about a watch that Lily may have given to someone? Say, to Bert?" Sam tried to jog her memory.

"A watch Lily gave Bert?" All of a sudden the older lady sat up straighter. "Yes, I do remember now. Lily gave Bert an old pocket watch she found. It was in terrible condition when she found it. I didn't think it was worth restoring, but she was determined." She peered at Sam and J.J. "But how did you figure out about the watch?"

Sam felt J.J. stiffen beside her. Should they tell her about their adventures of the night before?

J.J. interrupted before Sam could start. "We remembered, uh, a story, about how the head gardener years ago misplaced his watch."

"You mean George W..." Mrs. Goudy started to say.

"That's the one," Sam cut her off quickly. She didn't want her saying his name, in case they all flipped back in time. They still weren't sure if it only happened when they were on the Government House grounds. So far that had been the case, but she wasn't taking any chances. And she certainly didn't want to be responsible for Mrs. Goudy if they all went back!

"We got talking about it, and suddenly it made sense that Lily might be talking about a real watch," Sam explained.

Mrs. Goudy shrugged. "Makes as much sense as anything, I suppose."

"Do you remember where she found it?" J.J. asked.

"It was in 1941, I believe, because that's the year we had several special visitors," Mrs. Goudy said. "Lily came into the staff residence after work one day with this rusty old thing caked in dirt. She said she'd found it when she went to consult John Dewey about cutting flowers for the dining room and table."

"Do you remember her saying where exactly she found it?" J.J. asked.

Mrs. Goudy thought for a moment. "I remember we had huge sprays of pink roses and white chrysanthemums. She'd been out by the rose garden."

Sam nodded. "That makes sense." George Watt had been tending the roses the day they'd seen him without his watch. The flower bed seemed to still be in the same vicinity. But she wasn't going to tell Mrs. Goudy anything about their trips back in time.

"Sounds like it could be the gardener's," J.J. said.

"He was working near the rose garden the day his went missing," Sam added.

Mrs. Goudy stared at her. "How do you know so much detail?"

Oops, Sam had said too much. How could she know this much without admitting to being there when it happened?

J.J. came to her rescue. "There are all kinds of things in his old diaries."

"Yes, that's it," Sam said. At least J.J. hadn't said *they'd* read it in his diaries. She wasn't even sure he had written it there, but at least it seemed like a possible explanation. She turned a grateful smile on J.J.

"That may be one mystery solved," Sam said. "But I wonder what Lily wants us to know about it?"

"We may never know the answer to that one," Mrs. Goudy said.

"Have you seen Lily again?" J.J. asked, peering around the room.

"Not once," Mrs. Goudy said. "Though I feel more of her presence around me."

"Too bad she isn't here right now, so we could ask her what she wants us to know about the watch," Sam added.

Mrs. Goudy flashed them a grin. "Wouldn't that be a perfect world?"

"I wonder where the watch came from originally," J.J. said.

Sam jumped in. "I think it might have been a gift to the gardener before he left Scotland to come to Canada."

J.J. looked at her in astonishment.

Sam's eyes slid towards J.J. "Remember, we overheard the host or someone mention something about a Scottish duchess giving it to him?"

J.J. shook her head.

Sam hinted. "We heard about it the first time we, uh, explored the basement." On the sly, she mouthed 'seeing the mushrooms' to J.J.

J.J.'s face cleared. "Oh, right. I do remember hearing that."

Sam turned back to Mrs. Goudy. "Do you recall what the watch that Lily gave to Bert looked like?"

"The cover had some kind of Celtic design on it, leaves intertwined or something, but I really couldn't describe it for sure." She snapped her fingers. "But I do remember the motto engraved on the back. 'Tout Prest' – 'Quite Ready.'"

"We should be able to find something about it on the internet," J.J. said.

"Probably," Sam said. "But I'm not sure it will help us figure out what Lily wants us to know or do."

"Whatever happened to the watch?" J.J. asked. "Didn't you say Lily and Bert broke up after she gave it to him? Did he keep it?"

"Yes, they did break up shortly after that," Mrs. Goudy said. "And he went off to fight in the war. World War II, that would have been. And then he died on a muddy battlefield."

"How sad," Sam said. "Lily and Bert never had a chance to get back together."

"No, she was married to someone else by then anyway, so it wouldn't have ever come about." Mrs. Goudy shifted in her chair.

"At least we have a good idea that the watch the gardener lost is probably the same one that Lily found." J.J. looked pleased.

"We don't know they're the same for sure," Sam said. She glanced at J.J. "Wouldn't it be great if we could prove it?"

"I doubt you ever could without seeing both watches," Mrs. Goudy said.

Sam raised a knowing eyebrow at J.J.

With lips clenched tight, J.J. scowled at Sam.

Sam looked at the determined expression on J.J.'s face.

She knew J.J. would refuse to go, and she sure wasn't going to the past on her own. She wasn't even sure she wanted to go back again, even with J.J. beside her. But how else could they find out?

They sat in silence for a few minutes.

"Didn't you say the museum and interpretive centre had displays and information about the staff who worked here?" Mrs. Goudy asked. "Especially about the gardener, George..."

"Yes," J.J. and Sam chorused, before she could finish his full name.

"Maybe there'd be a clue there about at least one of them," Mrs. Goudy sighed. "But that's a long shot, and fairly useless unless you had information on the other one too."

"They have photographs and artifacts," J.J. agreed. "We might get lucky."

"At least it's a place to start." Sam looked at the clock. Almost 4:15 p.m. She jumped up. "If we hurry, we could get there before they close."

"Certainly. You go right ahead. I have to get ready to go out too." Mrs. Goudy waved them off. "Let me know how you make out."

"We will," Sam said, with J.J. trailing behind her out the door.

As they scampered down the hall, Sam kept a look out for Lily, but she didn't appear. At the entrance, Sam turned to J.J. "Your face is all red and blotchy. Are you feeling all right? Do you want to go home, or go to Government House with me?"

"Just tired. Do you think we'll find anything?"

"I want to look at the photograph of Geo...of *you know*

who," Sam said. "Maybe we can see details of his watch. Or maybe one of the hosts might know somewhere else to look that could help us."

J.J. gave Sam a reassuring smile. "That shouldn't take long, and it is right next door. We might as well go now. I'll be fine."

Inside Government House, they waved at the commissionaire inside the reception area and hurried to the conservatory. A display with a photo of George stood in the foyer. Although they could see the chain of his watch hanging out of his vest pocket, the timepiece wasn't visible. The write-up with the photo didn't mention anything about him coming from Scotland, but the gardener himself had mentioned it.

Though disappointed, they moved from room to room through the grand mansion, stopping at each display board to read about the staff who had worked in the area. Sam half-expected to see Jocko, the ghost monkey that belonged to Forget, swinging from the chandelier, or Cheun Lee shuffling about upstairs. She kept an eye out for the other ghosts they'd met before as well, but all seemed normal.

"I don't think we're going to find what we want here," J.J. said. She strayed into the billiards room, and then wandered back out to the ballroom to look at the ceremonial sword.

"I guess not," Sam said, ascending the carpeted staircase. "Let's head to the interpretive centre."

On the second floor, they took time to look at the artifacts in the bedrooms and read the display signs, searching for anything that might help. Then they crossed the hall quickly to the nurseries and governess' room.

"Wait a minute," Sam said, stopping in front of a display board near the balustrade. It showed a photo with several staff members. "Isn't that Alice as a housemaid, here in this picture?"

J.J. jostled in next to her. "I think that's Lily in the background too. Yes, both Lily and Alice are in this photograph."

The scene wobbled. Sam reached for J.J. as the display board disappeared.

IN FRONT OF THEM, green leafy garlands with red ribbons and bows decorated the banisters. Along the walls of the upper main hall, baskets of poinsettias and tiny Christmas figurines sat on the bookcase and chiffonier. The upper part of a Christmas tree poked through the centre well from the ballroom below. On its top perched a porcelain angel in a long white gown.

"Thanks for giving me a hand with the bedding," a female voice said from a guest bedroom across the hall. "We only got word that they would be arriving later tomorrow, but I didn't want to do the work on Christmas morning."

J.J. gaped at Sam, and then looked for a place to hide.

"Not a problem, Alice. That's what sisters are for. We still have plenty of time before we are to join the others in the ballroom for some fun. If we're done here, I'll see you downstairs in a few minutes. I just want to run a comb through my hair." Lily's shoes clacked on the hardwood floor as she walked across the room.

J.J. and Sam ducked into a small room in front of them

as Lily emerged from the bedroom across the hall. J.J. jammed herself against the wall and pulled Sam tight beside her, listening to Lily's muted descent down the carpeted stairs. They could hear Alice humming in the bedroom in time to the swish and shake of a dust mop.

J.J. looked aghast at Sam. "How did we shift to the past this time?" J.J. felt her skin get clammy.

"And how did we end up here in the 1940s again? We're not anywhere near that piece of foundation or the staff's quarters."

"Did we do something different?" J.J. asked.

"I think we just said their names," Sam said.

"Should we try that?" asked J.J.

J.J. poked her head out of the room. A tall woman swished by in a three-quarter-length, rose-coloured gown, with a chiffon scarf and a whiff of perfume.

"All done, Alice?" the woman called out as she passed Alice at the doorway of the guest bedroom.

"Yes, Mrs. McNab." She clicked off the light and followed the older lady down the stairs.

Sam drew back inside the room. "I guess we could try saying their names to get back." She added a little wistfulness to her voice. "Though I wouldn't mind taking a closer look, seeing as how we *are* here."

Seeing J.J.'s stunned look, she hastened to add, "But only if you want to, J.J."

"I don't know." J.J. poked her head around the corner and back again. "There are people everywhere. And they'll be able to see us."

"What if we just take a peek over the railing into the ballroom? I'd like to see the whole Christmas tree and how they decorated down there."

J.J. sighed. "Your quick peeks always get us into trouble."

"You just say the word, and we'll leave," Sam said. "Or attempt to," she added in a lower voice.

"Okay, but don't let go of my hand." J.J. grabbed Sam's fingers.

They tiptoed to the edge of the railing, knelt down and eased their faces between the posts. The Christmas tree in the ballroom below sparkled with gold ribbons, shiny silver balls, and tiny, white, lace-crocheted shapes. Red velvet poinsettia flowers were strategically placed all over the tree and were set off with loops of shimmering pearls. Warmth spread through J.J. as she surveyed the scene below.

They ducked back a little when Kate came in carrying a huge bowl of red punch. She set it in the middle of the table beside the staircase. Lily followed with a tray of glass cups that she arranged on hooks around the bowl. Alice brought in two large steaming teapots. Kate returned with a tray of teacups, a creamer and a sugar bowl.

One of the men came in and inserted a roll of music into the player piano and began pumping the pedals. Soon a Christmas song drifted across the ballroom.

"How beautiful," J.J. said. She wished she could sing along.

After a couple of songs, the man turned some kind of switch, and the piano continued to play, even though he'd quit pumping and walked away. J.J. and Sam watched as the perforated paper of the song rolls fed into the piano.

J.J. strained to see the various people as they entered the ballroom. Lieutenant Governor McNab and his wife greeted each of their staff members with a handshake, hug, or quick kiss on the cheek. Sam recognized some of the people as those they had met when they'd time-shifted, and some from photographs at Mrs. Goudy's. Bert was missing, though, so he must have quit by then.

Those remaining were dressed in what must have been their finest, bedecked with jewelry. The men had their hair tidy and slicked back, and the women had theirs done in curls, waves and fashionable rolls. When they were seated, Mr. McNab spoke a few words of thanks and wished them a joyous season.

Mrs. McNab helped her husband hand small, gaily-wrapped presents to each one.

"You may begin," he said, making sure everyone had a gift. "Open your gifts." Excitement shone in his eyes.

"Not before we give you yours, Your Honours – Archie, Edith," said Ruby. She rose and carried two brightly decorated boxes to the McNabs. "This is from all of us." Everyone clapped and wished them a wonderful Christmas.

Laughter and chiding rang out, as the McNabs took their time unwrapping their gifts.

"Don't wait for us," he said with a mischievous smile. "We might decide to take all night."

Soon everyone set about unwrapping their gifts, revealing jewelry, trinkets, hair barrettes, handkerchiefs, woolen gloves, and tie clips for the men. Lily and Alice showed each other the delicate hair combs they'd received: an ivory-coloured one to show off Lily's dark curls and a copper-coloured one to flatter Alice's blonde hair. Oohs and aahs and thank yous were called out across the room.

The McNabs had at last opened their gifts and held

them up high for all to see.

"What a beautiful shawl. Thank you everyone," Mrs. McNab wrapped a gold-threaded white shawl around her shoulders and sashayed for them.

Lieutenant Governor McNab tugged on his new fur-lined leather gloves. "Now we can have a proper snowball fight," he said with a hoot of laughter.

The women challenged the men to one the next day.

Watching the scene, J.J. felt a warm glow. Beside her, Sam gave a contented sigh.

"How about some punch?" Mrs. McNab rose and headed to the refreshment table.

"Let me serve, Mrs. McNab," said Kate, arriving with a tray of dainties, followed by Lily with another tray.

"Nonsense, it's our party for you." She shooed Kate away. "Go enjoy yourself."

J.J. gaped at the table laden with sweets. She spied flower-shaped shortbread cookies with shiny, silver, candy centres and lacy brandy snaps like her great-grand-mother used to make.

"Look, there are the gingerbread cookies," Sam said. "Just like Mrs. Goudy said."

J.J. stared at them hungrily. Nestled beside them was a stack of dark fruit cake with white icing. There were little sandwiches too, with baby gherkins. Her stomach gurgled. She clutched it and swallowed hard.

"We've got to get going. It's our supper time," J.J. said, crawling back from the railing.

"Watching this made me totally forget everything," Sam said as she slid back towards the wall next to J.J. "How wonderful it is to see how things actually were back then."

J.J. agreed. "Too bad we can't stay longer."

Sam glanced at J.J. "Your face is all flushed and blotchy. We have to get you home to bed."

"If we're lucky enough to get back," J.J. said, standing up and grabbing Sam's hand.

She gave Sam a quick glance, and without waiting for a response, said, "Alice and Lily."

Nothing happened.

J.J. gave Sam a shocked look. "Oh no."

J.J. felt a quiver of fear run up her back to the top of her neck. She had no idea how to get home. Were they going to be trapped in the past after all? What were they going to do?

CHAPTER NINE

"Quick! Someone's coming." Sam pulled J.J. back into the small room.

Light footsteps rushed up the staircase and paused just outside the room where they were hiding.

Sam held her breath. The footsteps moved into the next room. She heard a drawer slide open, then the sound of paper rustling.

While they waited for the person to leave, Sam glanced at the lacy hoar frost designs on the windows. She'd forgotten it must be winter outside. She felt a sudden chill.

At last, footsteps crept past them again and down the stairs. J.J. peeked out.

Sam breathed a sigh of relief. "Did you see who it was?"

"Ruby, I think," J.J. said.

"She must live in the house to be close to Mrs. McNab, if she's her companion," Sam said.

"Makes sense," J.J. said. "So what do we do now? We can't stay stuck back here."

"Let's think about the other times we shifted in time."

"Well, we were either touching some part of a building

or foundation, or we said people's names," J.J. said.

"Obviously saying their names doesn't work, and there's no part of a building or foundation to touch here, so that can't happen." Sam tapped her finger on her mouth and looked around.

"Not unless we go outside in the snow and try," J.J. said.

"For some reason, I don't think that's going to work this time." Sam sucked in her lip, trying to think.

"So what was different this time?" J.J. asked.

Sam reviewed the steps they'd taken. "Maybe if we stood exactly where we were before?"

They crept over beside the balustrade.

Sam took J.J.'s hand. She closed her eyes.

"Alice and Lily," she said.

She opened her eyes – they were still in the past.

"Lily and Alice," J.J. said their names in the opposite order.

Nothing.

Sam clenched her teeth. "There's something different. What is it?"

"Alice and Lily were up here too," J.J. said, "not far away from us."

"That could be it," Sam said hopefully. Then she slumped again. "How will we ever get the two of them up here together? They don't live in any of these upstairs rooms."

J.J. took a peek over the balustrade. "Maybe we have to go down to them," she said in a small voice.

"With all those people? How will we explain ourselves? They'll think we're thieves, or worse." Sam looked aghast at J.J.

J.J. squirmed under her glare. "Maybe we could get outside somehow and knock on the door. We could ask for them then."

Sam frowned. "How are we going to get past them and outside? The staircase leads right to them."

"There has to be another way out. What would they do in case of fire on the staircase?"

Sam thought for a minute, and then began tiptoeing into each of the rooms with J.J. on her heels. As quietly as they could, they examined the windows for possible routes of escape. The morning room windows opened onto a balcony, but there was no way down the two-storey drop.

"We're lucky that player piano is still going strong to cover the sound of our footsteps," Sam said when they'd made the full round of the second floor. They stood in the hallway outside the small room again.

All of a sudden, Sam pointed to a door in the upper hallway, just past the top of the grand staircase. In their own time the door was usually locked and had a keypad – it was a private entrance to the offices. But there was nothing locking it now.

"I wonder where that goes?" she asked, sidling over to it.

"Didn't it lead past Cheun Lee's room when he lived here?" J.J. recalled.

"You're right. Maybe it's Kate's room, now that she's the cook."

Sam edged over to the door. She peeked down the main staircase to make sure no one could see her. She tried the knob. It turned. J.J. patted her on the back, and they slipped through the doorway, closing it softly behind them.

Although it was dark, there was a small glow of light, and Sam could make out a short, narrow staircase that led downwards. They crept down the stairs to a landing with a room off of it.

"This must have been Chuen Lee's room," J.J. said. The door was ajar, but it was too dark to see inside. A light glowed from around a corner and down a second short staircase.

"I think we should go down this way." Sam took the lead. "The staircase must lead to the kitchen somehow, and we know we can get outside that way."

Sam and J.J. eased themselves down the dark stairway. Sam was heartened by the glow of light at the bottom that helped guide them.

"Good work, Sam," J.J. said, as they stepped into the brightly lit kitchen.

Pulling their hoodies tight around them, they scampered across the tile floor and made it to the back vestibule and out the door. A gust of cold wind hit them, and they found themselves up to their ankles in snow.

As Sam stamped the snow off her feet, she asked, "Do you think we should go around to the front door?"

"That's the ceremonial entrance, only for special guests," J.J. said with alarm.

"I don't know if they'll hear us knocking from here." Sam nodded towards the house. They could hear music and laughter from deep inside. "We don't really have much of a choice."

"Whatever we do, we have to do it fast. Otherwise, we'll freeze out here and never get home." J.J. jumped up and down to keep warm.

"Okay. Let's go."

They ran around the corner of the house and were almost thrown back by another heavy gust of wind. Blowing snow whirled into their faces as they sprinted to the next corner, thrashing through drifts of snow to reach the front of the building.

As they rounded the last corner, Sam slipped and fell. Jabs of pain shot through her bad knee. She limped up against the building to catch her breath. "The same knee," she gasped.

J.J. stopped beside her, breathing hard in the blustery night. "Only a little way to go. Can you make it?"

The worry on J.J.'s face made Sam want to cry. "I'll be fine." She took a deep breath.

J.J. put her arm around Sam's waist and they stumbled to the portico as another blast of wind hit them. J.J. stomped up to the door and banged the heavy knocker as loud as she could. Sam leaned against the doorframe, sucking back the pain in her knee and holding her hoodie tight around her face.

J.J. kept banging. At last someone opened the door. A blast of warmth hit them.

"It's the two waifs from the summer, isn't it?" Ernie said, when he caught sight of them.

Sam nodded.

"What on earth are you doing out on a night like this?" he asked, as several glanced their way. Sam stared at the faces, searching for Alice and Lily. They had to get them alone.

"Bring them in, dear fellow," said Archie McNab, who had joined them at the door. "Then we can sort things out."

As Ernie ushered them into the foyer, Lily was the first

to step forward.

"You're the one who remembered me from my picture." She scrutinized them from head to toe. "You're wearing trousers. And your footwear is very different. You're not from around these parts, are you?"

Alice came up to them and said, "My goodness, you're not dressed nearly warm enough for a night like this. You must be freezing. Let's get you by some heat, and then we can talk."

Sam and J.J. started to untie their laces.

"Leave your, uh, shoes on," Lily said, staring at their runners with the neon lightning bolts.

Sam and J.J. wiped the bottom of their runners on the thick mat at the door and Lily escorted them across the ballroom. Sam's feet felt squishy in her wet socks and runners as they crossed the hardwood floor. She glanced quickly at J.J. She seemed to be walking a little awkwardly too.

When they passed a group standing around Archie McNab, he raised his eyebrows. "Looks like you two have things under control."

"Yes," said Lily. "We'll get some hot tea into them and make sure they get home."

"I'll let you take care of them then." He turned back to the others. "Come on. Let's play charades."

Everyone dispersed with an air of joviality. As Lily walked towards the drawing room, her below-the-knee, green party dress swished. Alice's red dress was more fitted with buttons, down to a narrow waist and straight skirt. Her blonde, curled hair bounced with her every step.

Lily seated them on a couch near the hot air vents. "I'll

get some tea."

Lily left and Alice followed, saying, "I'll get blankets."

Sam glanced at J.J. with a grim smile. "Well, we've made it in. Do you think we need to take them back upstairs, where we were shifted into this time?"

J.J. rubbed her hands up and down her arms and thought for a moment. "We moved around quite a bit when we were back with, uh, *you know who*, so I don't think we have to be up there again."

"Should we just say their names right here?" Sam sat hunched and shivering.

"What will they think if we disappear before their eyes? And in front of all of these other people?" J.J. asked.

"I don't see any other way of doing it. And we've got to get back soon." Sam leaned closer to the heating vents, rubbing her hands.

"Let's see if we can get them to the doorway at least," J.J. suggested.

"Good idea," Sam said. "Let's have a quick cup of tea to warm up and then go."

Lily arrived first with cups of hot tea and a ginger-bread cookie perched on each saucer. She set the red, rose-flowered teacups on a low table in front of them.

"Thank you." Sam wrapped her hands around the delicate teacup and took a small swallow of tea.

J.J bit into the cookie. "Mmm, this is really good. The gingerbread seems to melt in my mouth."

"I'm glad you like them," Lily said.

Alice arrived soon afterwards and wrapped a thick wool blanket around each of them.

She and Lily sat in straight-backed chairs across from them, hands clasped in their laps.

"First, dears, what are your names?" Lily asked.

"I'm Samantha and this is Jensyn," Sam said.

"Unusual, but pretty names," Alice said.

"You can call us J.J. and Sam," J.J. offered.

"Thank you, we'll remember that," Lily said, her blue eyes twinkling.

"And you're Lily," Sam said.

J.J. greeted the other woman. "And you must be Alice." The two women looked surprised.

"How did you know?" Lily asked.

"We heard your names, uh..." Sam sputtered.

"Someone told us who you were in a photograph," J.J. said.

"Oh yes, the photograph you mentioned," Lily said. Alice looked puzzled.

"One of the two of you," J.J. said, taking a sip of tea.

"Taken outside in the grounds by a hedge," Sam said.

"That was taken last summer," Lily said with a baffled expression. "But how on earth would you have seen it?"

Sam was stumped. She had no possible answer. She shrugged. "I don't remember." She felt herself going red in the face.

J.J. shook her head and sat in silence.

Sam didn't know what to say. What must the women be thinking about them? She bowed her head.

"It is curious," Alice said, "but we're embarrassing the girls. So tell us, how old are you?"

"Ten," J.J. said, nibbling at her cookie.

"Both of you?" Lily re-secured the ivory-coloured comb in her dark hair.

Sam nodded. After a few bites of cookie and more swallows of tea, Sam felt warm again, though her socks were wet and her feet still cold.

"Now, tell us, what brings you here?" Lily asked with a kind smile.

"And on a stormy Christmas Eve," Alice said, her brown eyes bright. "You're not lost, are you?"

Sam shook her head. J.J. squirmed beside her. They had to say something.

J.J. set her tea cup down on the saucer, clattering it only a little. "We saw the beautiful Christmas tree through the window and wanted to see it close up."

Saved by J.J. again. Sam breathed a little easier and reached for another cookie. They *were* really good.

"In a storm like this?" Sam heard Alice asking.

"It wasn't storming when we first decided to come," Sam said, thinking of the fall afternoon they'd left behind. Sam unzipped her hoodie.

Lily scrutinized them again.

"Where do you live?"

"I bet you came from somewhere else to visit family for the holiday?" Alice guessed.

"No, we live just across the Avenue," Sam said, her mind whirring. They were asking too many questions. They had to leave soon.

Lily and Alice exchanged glances.

"Do your parents know you're here?" Alice asked with concern.

"Not *here*, they don't." J.J. clenched her hands in her lap.

"They knew we were going for walk," Sam added hastily. "It's something we often do."

"But before they worry, we really need to get back home." J.J. sat up straighter. "Yes, we'd better hurry."

"But it's storming out," Alice protested. "We'll telephone your folks and let them know you're safe here with us until someone from the R.C.M.P. can escort you home."

"You can't phone our parents," Sam said, bolting upright.

"And you don't need to call the police," J.J. said with a squeak, as she zipped up her hoodie.

"I already called," Alice said. "Constable Roup should be here in another few minutes."

Sam looked over at J.J., who had a terrified look in her eyes.

"We live really close by," Sam said. "We'll just go now and be home right away." She shrugged the blanket off, jumped up and began zipping up her hoodie. J.J. stood up beside her.

"We really should telephone your parents to let them know you're on your way. Aren't they on a line?" Lily raised her eyebrows.

J.J. shook her head.

"Uh no, well, the line is down right now." Sam crossed her fingers behind her back, hoping they'd believe what she said. Thoughts tumbled in Sam's head. She didn't know if everyone had telephones back then, but there was no way they could dial any of their current numbers.

Alice and Lily glanced at one another with worried looks.

"It's better if we just get back right away." J.J. started edging towards the ballroom.

"We'll be home in no time," Sam said, right behind J.J. They sure didn't want to see Constable Roup again after he'd witnessed their last "disappearing act."

"At least let us get one of the men to walk with you," Alice said. She glanced into the ballroom where the others played charades.

"Oh no, we'll be fine on our own," Sam protested.

"We live really, really close," J.J. insisted. "We'll be together."

J.J. edged farther into the ballroom, with Sam right behind her.

"Though it would be nice if you both could just walk us to the door," Sam said, keeping her fingers crossed that just the two of them would come. If they could get Alice and Lily over to the door and leave through it, it might seem more natural when they disappeared – if their plan worked.

"We'll certainly do that," Lily said. "But we really think you ought to wait for an escort."

Sam and J.J. quickened their pace across the ballroom, back to the front vestibule, with Alice and Lily following them.

"Goodbye girls. Merry Christmas," Mr. McNab and the others called out as they passed the group of partiers.

"Goodbye," Sam and J.J. chorused. Sam was grateful no one else joined them.

At the door, Sam and J.J. stood together, shoulders touching. Sam sure hoped their plan worked, and before the RCMP arrived.

"You've been very nice to us. Thank you," J.J. said, shaking each of their hands in turn.

Sam followed suit. "Yes, thank you. It was very nice to meet you."

"Thanks for the cookies and tea," J.J. added.

"You're welcome, dears," Alice said.

"Maybe we'll see you again sometime," Lily said.

"I'm fairly certain we will," J.J. muttered under her breath to Sam.

"That would be nice. Maybe we will," Sam said aloud. She hoped this worked; otherwise, they'd be seeing a whole lot more of the sisters, the McNabs, and their staff in the very next few minutes.

Sam pulled open the door to the wind whistling around the portico.

Alice and Lily shivered in the doorway, worried looks on their faces.

"We can see our house lights from here." Sam grabbed J.J.'s hand. "We'll be fine."

"Thank you again," Sam said, stepping outside, with J.J.'s hand firmly clenched in hers.

The snow whirled about them, as she nodded at J.J.

As Sam slammed the door shut, they called out together, "Goodbye, Alice and Lily."

Late afternoon sun filtered down on them from a darkish sky. The air was damp from the rain.

J.J. hugged Sam hard. "We did it."

Sam sagged against J.J. "I'm so glad we're back." She put her arm around J.J.'s waist, and her friend guided her down the path towards home.

CHAPTER TEN

"You're lucky some of the other kids didn't have their posters done yesterday either," J.J. said on their way home from school the next day.

"Mrs. Lindstrom's still docking a mark from each of us, to make it fair because we were late. But I deserve it," Sam said. "I didn't have any time to finish it until last night. I didn't do it at lunch or stay after school, like I'd planned."

"It isn't like you were goofing off entirely, though," J.J. said. "We were rather busy."

"That's for sure." Sam laughed. "I wonder how Alice and Lily took it when we disappeared so fast."

"You did slam the door in their faces," J.J. said.

"But it was stormy out," Sam said. "So, I'm sure they understood."

"Hopefully they didn't worry," J.J. said. "It's not like we could go back and tell them we're okay."

For a moment, Sam was silent beside her. "In a way, we could."

No! I don't want to go through that again! J.J. thought. She whirled on her friend and gave her shoulders a little shake. "Tell me, you're not planning on going back again." She stared into Sam's eyes.

Sam grimaced. "No way. Not after the way we got stuck in time last night."

"Good." J.J. let go of her friend.

"I was just thinking about the mystery of the watch. We still haven't proved it was the same one."

J.J. said, "Do you still think it's important to go to the interpretive centre? I'll go with you now, if you like."

"You're sure you're feeling okay?"

"I had a better sleep last night. I'm fine to go for a short time."

"You're the greatest, J.J." Sam hugged her friend. "I'd still like to check it out. I don't really know anywhere else to find anything out."

J.J. grinned. Sam always made her feel appreciated. They linked arms and raced to the Government House. They toned down their enthusiasm when they entered the foyer.

"Back so soon?" the commissionaire welcomed them.

"Just want to see a couple of things again," Sam said, standing in front of the counter.

He waved at them.

J.J. turned to Sam. "Let's take the back way to the interpretive centre," she suggested. "I don't want to go through the rest of the house today."

Sam agreed. "Especially not after the way we saw it last night. It was so pretty, all decorated for Christmas. But I still feel a little creeped out about how we left, even though it's daytime now."

They turned the opposite way from the commission-aire's desk and headed for the side stairwell, pumping up the stairs as fast as they could. On the second floor, they hustled along past the board room, offices, and through the art gallery, until they reached the back entrance to the interpretive centre. They were already familiar with the display rooms, and the Lieutenant Governors at Dinner Room, so they went straight to the exhibits.

J.J. and Sam sauntered around the space, studying the various artifacts on display in glass cabinets. No watch, though there were some interesting articles from the past. Standing next to Sam, J.J. read the small, hand-written cards describing each piece and where it came from.

"Can I help you find anything?" The visitor experience host, Robin, walked toward them, wearing a Victorian costume.

"We were just looking for things that might have belonged to the gardener from a long time ago," Sam said.

"Like a pocket watch," J.J. said as she leaned in for a closer look, brushing against Sam's shoulder.

Robin said, "That would be a nice addition. But which gardener?"

"George Watt," J.J. said without thinking. Then she gasped and grabbed Sam's arm.

Suddenly, they were standing in a sunny greenhouse, filled with brilliant-coloured flowers and leafy greenery. The air was humid.

"I'm sorry. It just slipped out." J.J. felt horrified. The mistake was entirely her fault.

"At least we can ask him directly about his watch," Sam said. She pointed towards the far end, where George stood watering a huge, potted fern.

"Maybe we don't really need to know. Let's get out of here," J.J. pleaded, but George had already caught sight of them.

"So you girls are back," he said with a tilt of his head. "I wondered where you got to."

"We had to get something we left outside the other day," J.J. blurted. "I guess you didn't hear us tell you."

He shrugged. "No matter. So what brings you to the greenhouse today?"

"We just wondered if you'd found your pocket watch yet?" Sam asked.

He shook his head. "I thought maybe I'd left it in my house, but it's not there. So I guess I lost it in the grounds. I've looked everywhere I worked that day, and even some places I didn't, but no luck."

"Did someone special give it to you?" J.J. asked. She might as well be direct.

"Didn't you say something about a duchess?" Sam said.

"You heard that, did you?" He laughed. "Yes, the Duchess of Atholl gave it to me when I left her employment as gardener. She hired me on as a junior gardener at Blair Castle – that was in Perthshire, Scotland."

"She must have been impressed with your gardening," Sam said.

George raised his eyebrows. "I suppose she was. I never expected a gift, much less a pocket watch of that calibre."

"What did it look like?" Sam asked.

"We know it was silver. But did it have a design on the cover, or any writing on it?" J.J. held her breath.

"The design on the case was a Celtic shield knot. Something to do with the Atholl clan ancestry, I believe." He chuckled. "The inscription was 'Tout Prest' – 'Quite Ready.' I guess that does show she had faith in my abilities as a gardener. Enough to send me off into the world, at any rate." George stood, deep in thought.

J.J. shared a smile with Sam. They had part of their answer. The watch Lily found and gave Bert had been George's. Too bad there wasn't some way of getting it back to Mr. Watt. They'd never be able to track it through Bert.

"I'm sorry you lost it," J.J. said.

"We'll keep our eyes out for it," Sam said.

"I appreciate that," said George. "Well, I must get these plants watered before the day turns too hot in here."

"We have to go too, uh, to do some, uh..." J.J. tried to think of something they would have had to do if they lived in that time period. "...needlework," she finished. She grabbed Sam's arm and whirled her about.

"Goodbye," Sam said over her shoulder, as J.J. rushed her out of the conservatory. George had already turned back to his watering.

At the door, J.J. stopped and looked Sam in the eyes.

Then she said in a soft voice. "Goodbye..."

Sam nodded.

They clasped hands, and together, they said, "George Watt."

Instantly, the visitor experience host stood in front of them with an alarmed look.

J.J. and Sam steadied each other.

"What just happened?" Robin stammered.

"I'm not sure what you mean," J.J. said. She shifted around the edge of the glass cabinet, trying to look innocent.

"You just disappeared and reappeared." Robin took a step back from them, her hands on her mouth.

"Maybe something to do with the reflections," Sam suggested.

The host continued to stare at them. "But, I'm sure you disappeared..."

Sam looked sideways at J.J. She shrugged at Robin. "I don't really know..."

"We have to get home now." J.J. adjusted her backpack and nudged Sam. "Thanks for your help."

"Yeah, thanks," Sam said, stepping past the shocked host and down the hall behind J.J. They didn't look back.

They pushed their way through the doors to the stairwell and clattered down the steps to the main entrance. Outside, they collapsed against each other, breathing hard.

Sam started laughing and couldn't stop.

J.J. giggled beside her. "This is getting a little crazy, with other people seeing us disappear," she said with a snort.

"As long as they don't start talking to each other, we're okay for now," Sam said, becoming serious again. "We'd never be able to explain it."

"They'd never believe us, even if we tried." J.J. took a drink of water from the bottle in her backpack. "I'm so glad we figured out the origins of the watch, and now we can forget about everything to do with all the ghosts." J.J. felt a little shiver run up her back. Were they really done? She hoped so.

"Sometime, we should let Mrs. Goudy know about the watch," J.J. suggested, flinging her backpack up into the air and catching it again.

"We could see if she's up for a visit right now," Sam said. "That is, if you're up for it?"

"Yes, I'm fine." J.J. gave her a thumbs up.

"I'll call," Sam flipped out her cell phone, punched in the numbers, and spoke for a few seconds.

"She's happy to see us," Sam said, putting away her phone.

They headed across the parking lot and into the building. Amber wasn't at the reception desk this time, so they breezed by. No sign of Lily either, until they reached Mrs. Goudy's suite. J.J. blinked and nudged Sam. Lily stood beside Mrs. Goudy's chair.

"There you are, my dears." Mrs. Goudy gestured for them to sit in their usual places. "So tell us what you've learned."

J.J. gave Mrs. Goudy a startled look. Did she realize who was beside her?

"Oh yes, I know Lily is here too." Mrs. Goudy laughed.

Sam recovered first. "We did a little research, and I was right. The pocket watch did belong to Geo..." J.J. threw Sam a warning look. "Uh, to the former gardener."

Between them, J.J. and Sam filled in the story for Mrs. Goudy, leaving out the details of the time travel, of course.

"How special," she said, clapping her hands when they'd finished. "If this is what Lily wanted us to know, the mystery is solved."

J.J. noticed that Lily's face still looked downcast. "I have the feeling that wasn't what Lily had in mind."

The others turned to Lily, and she shook her head a little.

"But I wonder what she wants us to do?" Sam asked.

She mouthed something.

"I think she said, 'Find the watch,'" J.J. said.

"I agree," Mrs. Goudy said.

Lily nodded.

Sam nodded. "But how?"

"And where?" J.J. asked.

Mrs. Goudy looked at her sister's ghost. "You never told me what you did with it after receiving it with Bert's belongings after the war. I don't know how to find it now."

Lily's shoulders sagged.

Sam bolted upright. "She got it back?"

"Yes, dears. Bert's effects were sent to Lily when he died. He had no other close relatives, and he had named her as his beneficiary."

With tears welling in her eyes, J.J. turned to the ghost. "He really loved you, didn't he?"

Lily nodded sadly.

"He was your true love," Mrs. Goudy said. "You loved your husband, but you loved Bert too."

Lily nodded again and stared at Alice for a moment. Then she glided closer to a photo on the wall and eyed it. The one of the light-haired young man Mrs. Goudy hadn't named.

Alice nodded. "Yes, he was my special true love – Gerard was his name, but it wasn't meant to be."

J.J. studied the photo of the handsome young man in uniform. So Mrs. Goudy had lost someone special too. Would she ever tell them about it? By the stoical set of her face, J.J. was sure she wouldn't.

J.J. turned quickly back to the conversation when she heard Sam ask, "What do you want us to do about the watch?"

Find the watch, Lily mouthed again.

"But where?" Sam asked.

Lily swept an arm out, pointing towards the Government House grounds. Her shape started to waver.

"Where out there?" J.J. called out frantically.

But Lily's ghost had disappeared.

❧

"How are we ever going to figure out where?" Sam turned to Mrs. Goudy.

Mrs. Goudy looked bewildered.

"Do you have any idea what she might have done with Bert's things?" J.J. asked.

Mrs. Goudy shook her head. "I don't know what she did. We were both married and living in different places by then. And she died not long afterwards."

Sam leaned towards Mrs. Goudy. "Do you have any of her belongings?"

Mrs. Goudy thought for a few moments. "The only thing I have left is her jewelry box."

"Maybe there's a clue in it," J.J. said.

"If so, I wouldn't know what it would be. There are only a few trinkets. But we can look if you like." She made a move as if to rise from her chair, but then she eased back down. "Why don't you get it, J.J.? It's tucked away in the bottom drawer of my dresser in the bedroom."

J.J. stood up. "Are you sure?"

"Yes, dear. It's on the right hand side, beside my winter sweaters."

J.J. emerged a short time later with a small wooden

box, intricately carved with flowers and vines. She set in on the table in front of Mrs. Goudy.

The elderly lady gently opened the clasped box and lifted the lid. The first thing they saw was the ivory hair comb.

Sam blurted, "The Christmas present Lily got from the McNabs."

Mrs. Goudy gave a little gasp. "How do you know that?"

Sam felt the colour drain out of her face. She stammered. "I thought, uh, I read a list somewhere, uh, of the gifts the McNabs gave their staff."

Mrs. Goudy stared at her oddly, and then glanced over at J.J. She closed her eyes for a few moments.

When she opened them, she spoke. "I remember the year the McNabs gave Lily and I these combs for Christmas. Lily was given this one and I was given a..."

"...copper-coloured one," Sam finished for her in a whisper.

Mrs. Goudy stared at them as she continued. "That Christmas Eve night, it started to storm, and two girls came to the door. We invited them in and gave them tea..."

"And gingerbread cookies," J.J. said.

"When they left, they disappeared abruptly. We couldn't figure out what happened to them. Not even Constable Roup could find them." Mrs. Goudy seemed to be puzzling something through in her mind.

Sam and J.J. sat very still.

"When I look at you now, I recall those girls looked very much like the two of you." She put her hand on her chest as if slowing her heartbeat. "The only reasonable explanation I can come up with for you knowing so much is that those two girls must have been your grandmothers when they were young."

"Wow," was all that Sam could think of to say. She felt her pulse racing. J.J. stayed mute beside her, though Sam could feel her friend trembling.

"Do you have anything more to say about this, or shall we agree that this is what happened, and your grandmothers told you the story?" Mrs. Goudy stared at them half uneasily, and half wistfully.

Sam nodded slowly. If Mrs. Goudy was willing to believe that, she was happy to let the discussion go.

"Sounds good to me," J.J. squeaked out.

Without another word, Mrs. Goudy chose things out of the jewelry box and laid them on the table. The girls handled each one carefully, as Mrs. Goudy explained what they were. Besides Lily's hair comb, there was an array of delicate earrings, necklaces and brooches, as well as an embroidered handkerchief edged in lace, and a well-used stick of lipstick. Plus, some medals.

"I forgot Bert's medals were in here. But no watch," Mrs. Goudy said, somewhat disappointedly. "But then I didn't really expect it would be. She must have done something with it, though."

"Would she have had it buried with him?"J.J. asked.

"No, dear. The men who died overseas during the war are buried near where they fell."

"May I see the box?" Sam asked.

Mrs. Goudy passed Sam the box, and she and J.J. continued to sort through the jewelry.

Sam caressed the elegant, carved designs on the outside. When she looked inside, she noticed the inside depth didn't match the outside. She held it up and turned it this way and that.

"Have you found something I've missed?" Mrs. Goudy asked.

"I'm not sure. I think there might be a false bottom in it." Sam passed the box to Mrs. Goudy.

"I do believe you're right, though I have no idea how to open it." Mrs. Goudy tried pushing a few of the carved flowers on the outside, but nothing happened.

"Let me see if I can figure it out," J.J. said. "There must be a hidden trigger." She examined the outside carefully, and then passed it back to Sam.

Sam pressed each side of the interior surfaces, and then flipped the box over to examine the bottom. All at once, the bottom released, and sprang up enough for her to get her fingers along the back edge. When she drew up the bottom panel, she found a stained photograph tucked in the hidden portion.

"Wow." Sam gazed at the photo in amazement for a few moments, and then handed it to Mrs. Goudy.

"Lily and Bert. They're sitting in their favourite spot in the grounds," Mrs. Goudy said. Her face was sad. "This must have been right after she gave him the watch."

Sam and J.J. leaned over her shoulder to take a better look. The couple was sitting on a wrought iron bench in front of a rose garden. Climbing rose vines grew up and over a trellis that sheltered the bench. They were both smiling and leaning slightly into one another. Bert held the watch in his hand between them, and Lily had her hand cupped under his.

Sam perked up. "Did you say this was their favourite spot?"

"They spent hours out there when they had free time," Mrs. Goudy said. "Lily loved the scent of the roses and, in those days, the bench was sheltered from the wind and the sun, in a cove of caragana bushes."

All of a sudden, Sam noticed some writing on the back of the photograph. "What does it say on the back?" she asked.

Mrs. Goudy read the inscription out loud. "Together for all time."

J.J.'s mouth fell open.

"Are you thinking what I'm thinking?" Sam asked.

"She buried the watch again," J.J. guessed.

"In the rose garden," added Sam.

Mrs. Goudy's eyes widened. "By golly, it would be just like her to do that."

"But the rose garden is really big. We couldn't possibly dig it all up." J.J. wiggled to the edge of her seat.

"And it's already been dug up lots of times over the years, and probably moved a little too," Sam said.

J.J. frowned. "Someone probably already found the watch by now."

"But then why does Lily want us to find it? She probably wouldn't ask us to find it if someone else had it. What would it matter?" Sam asked.

"I don't think someone found it, either," Mrs. Goudy said. "Roses...hmmm..." Mrs. Goudy seemed lost in thought.

Sam and J.J. thought hard too.

All at once, an idea jumped into Sam's mind. "Not that rose garden."

"Huh?" J.J. stared at her friend.

"We keep thinking it's the big rose garden where

Geo..." Sam stopped short. "Where *you* know *who* lost his watch. But what if Lily didn't put it in the same place as she found it?"

Sam swooped up the photo of Lily and Bert. "What if it's by another rose garden? This doesn't look like the same one." At least, it didn't look like the one they'd seen when they'd gone back to the past.

"You're right it doesn't," J.J. said. She tapped the photo. "There wasn't a trellis there."

Mrs. Goudy stared at them. "How do you...?"

"You don't want to know," Sam said, "but trust us, we know."

Mrs. Goudy nodded. "There was a smaller garden where Lily and Bert always went. It makes perfect sense that she'd think to bury the watch there."

"At least it should be a smaller area to search," Sam said.

"But we don't even know where the garden was, and it is still be too big an area to dig ," J.J. said.

"But it's a place to start." Sam turned towards Mrs. Goudy. "Can you help us figure out exactly where this one was?"

Mrs. Goudy pursed her lips. "It was so long ago, and it's been gone for years. Other than it being northeast of the staff building, I couldn't pinpoint it. I'm really sorry, but I don't think I can help you this time."

Sam and J.J. slumped back. Mrs. Goudy looked disappointed.

"I guess there's nothing more we can do," Sam said glumly. "Without Lily telling us, we're hooped."

"But that's okay," J.J. said to Mrs. Goudy. "It was a long shot anyway."

Sam agreed. "We're thankful for all the help you've been able to give us."

But Sam knew they needed to find the watch somehow; otherwise, she and J.J. would keep popping back and forth in time. If only they'd been able to follow Bert and Lily around the corner of the staff residence, instead of being flipped back to the present. They probably would have seen the bench and rose garden for themselves. How could they solve this dilemma when they had no idea where the rose garden had been? Would they ever find the watch or know why locating it was so important?

Sam made up her mind. She and J.J. had to try.

CHAPTER ELEVEN

"I'm so sorry to disappoint you," Mrs. Goudy said.

She looked so mournful, that J.J. leaned over and gave her a hug. "It's okay."

"If only Lily would appear and guide us," Sam said wistfully.

"She only seems to appear when she wants to, not when we need her, just like how she was in person," Mrs. Goudy said with a little smile.

J.J. glanced around Mrs. Goudy's suite.

"Would talking about it help? Maybe something will twig your memory," J.J. asked.

"Even if you know sort of where the small garden was, we might be able to figure something out," Sam suggested.

"I could start with what I *do* know about it, but I don't think it will be of much use," Mrs. Goudy said.

"How about where it was compared to the staff quarters? Was it close by? Who used it?" J.J. asked.

"That's easy. Mostly the staff used it, although sometimes Mrs. McNab went out there too, because it was more private than the bigger garden to the east." Mrs. Goudy drew herself upright. "It would have been east and north of the northeast corner of our residence. I recall that the landscaping was symmetrical at that time, so the centres of the two rose gardens would have lined up with one another."

"Great," J.J. said.

Sam asked, "Could you maybe draw a diagram of where you think it was?"

"I suppose I could give you a rough idea, but I doubt I can pinpoint it exactly."

"That's all right." Sam drew her notebook out of her backpack and flipped it open. J.J. handed her a pen from her hoodie pocket.

"You already know where the foundation to the staff quarters was, or at least part of it," Mrs. Goudy said, almost to herself.

J.J. and Sam nodded.

Deftly, Mrs. Goudy sketched the staff residence, the caragana hedge, and the wooden sidewalk. Then she drew a line for the edge of the grounds at Dewdney Avenue and added the current maintenance road and the large rose garden. She sat back in thought.

"I'm almost certain that the northeast corner of the building was in line with the north edge of the parking lot, close to where we are now in Pioneer Village. So that should give you an idea of where the one edge of the residence was."

J.J. laughed. "See, your memory is just fine."

Mrs. Goudy chuckled. "I only recall that the edge of the servant's quarters lined up with the edge of the parking lot. That's because when I first came to live here twenty years ago, I walked over to see the bit of foundation where I once lived on the grounds. I noted the sightline. As I was drawing, I remembered."

She peered back down at the diagram. "I'm fairly certain it was forty feet square. I'm not sure how far the small flower bed was from the northeast corner of the staff building, but I know that it lay about halfway between it and the carriage road into the grounds."

She talked to herself. "Maybe about here. No, that's not right," she muttered. "I used to sit there and wait for the streetcar."

Mrs. Goudy glanced up at them. "You could see it coming from a long ways off, so it had to be farther to the northeast."

"Wow, what great detail," Sam said.

Mrs. Goudy sat with her eyes closed for a few moments. When she opened them again, she said, "My best guess, is that the small rose garden would be about here." She marked it on the diagram. "That's still a fairly large space to search."

"Was there anything else in the area we could use as a landmark?" Sam asked.

"Not really." Mrs. Goudy shook her head. "The only thing around there were the caragana hedges – long gone now – and some elm trees." She started to smile. "There were two trees, each with a branch sticking out at right angles from their trunks. They were so odd looking, and scary at times. We used to joke that they were a young couple reaching out for one another."

"Were the trees close to the rose garden?" J.J. sat up with a brainwave. "They might still be there...just bigger now."

Mrs. Goudy laughed. "I'm sure they're probably still growing." She drew them where she thought they had been. "The bench was on a forty-five degree angle facing northeast towards Dewdney Avenue. When I sat there, I could see the gate posts to the carriage road between the two trees."

Sam gave J.J. the thumbs up. "We're narrowing the location down."

"Any idea of the distance of the garden from the corner of the staff residence or from the gate?" J.J. asked.

"No, but I know it was thirty steps from the bench to the tree on the left, with the odd branch sticking out. I purposely paced it out one day when I was waiting for a streetcar that was late." Mrs. Goudy seemed pleased to have remembered that detail.

"You've given us some great information to go on," J.J. said. "We should be able to find the rose garden now."

"But where the watch might be buried, I have no idea." Mrs. Goudy looked sad again.

"Maybe we could figure it out from this." Sam picked up the photograph again.

"Was there something particular they could see from where they sat?" J.J. asked, peering over Sam's shoulder.

"What do you think, Mrs. Goudy?" Sam asked. "Was their anything interesting to notice at the rose garden, or anything you think would have been special for them there?"

"Not a thing I can think of." She studied the photograph.

J.J. watched her face change expression several times over the next few minutes.

At last she spoke. "I knew Lily fairly well, and I'm guessing she would have wanted the watch to be close to where they always sat. But not a place too obvious to others who might notice that the earth had been disturbed. I'd bet it had to be right around the bench somewhere."

"She probably wouldn't have buried it where it was difficult to get to, so I'd say it wouldn't be underneath the bench," Sam said.

"I agree," Mrs. Goudy said.

J.J. turned to her and asked, "Where would you put it, if you were her?"

Without hesitation Mrs. Goudy spouted, "I'd dig right behind the bench, somewhere about the middle. Probably where they would have sat. No one else would see the spot when they sat there. The arbor vines and flowers would hide the spot too. Yet, it would be right there, where they spent so much time together."

"Then that's the spot where we should start," Sam said.

J.J. said, "Great. Now all we have to do is find the *exact* spot where the bench used to be."

"That's not *all* we have to do," Sam hesitated. "I'm not sure anyone's going to let us go digging around the grounds."

"Unless you start digging big holes everywhere, no one is likely to notice. Besides, if you find it, you would give it to the museum," Mrs. Goudy said.

"But wouldn't it belong to you?" J.J. asked.

Mrs. Goudy tilted her head and frowned. "I'm not sure. If you find it on the Government House grounds, it might belong to them. Besides, I have no use for it, and others might as well enjoy it, especially if it once belonged to the original landscaper – *you know who* – of the grounds."

J.J. grinned at Mrs. Goudy's use of their term for

George Watt.

"*If* we find it," Sam said. "We don't even know if we've figured out the right place. Or if she even buried it. All we can do is try."

J.J. looked at Mrs. Goudy. "How deep do you think it would be buried?"

"Probably just a little more than the length of a spade. The gardeners would have dug the soil by hand back then, and Lily wouldn't need to go too much deeper. They probably didn't have a need to dig around the bench that much, anyway."

"The ground is really packed now," Sam said.

J.J. remembered how hard it was to scrape away the soil from the foundation with her pencil. "What could we use to dig with?"

"A shovel is too big and obvious, but my mom has a trowel," Sam said. "I could get it."

"I have one from when I used to keep potted plants," Mrs. Goudy said. "Take a look in the closet." Mrs. Goudy motioned for her to search for it.

As SAM DUG around in the closet, the clock chimed five times. She and J.J. still had a bit of time before they had to be home for supper. She clattered through a box of old tools and spied the trowel.

When she returned with it, Mrs. Goudy laughed. "That should do it. Finally it's being used again, and for a good cause."

"Do you think it's okay if we go dig right now?"

"Why not?" Mrs. Goudy shrugged with an impish

grin. "It's after five, and the commissionaire will have gone home, and all the staff. If you don't find anything, well then, no harm done, and if you do, there's plenty of time to alert someone tomorrow."

Sam glanced at J.J. "Are you feeling okay enough to do this?"

"Sure, let's go," she said.

"Wish I was able to come with you," Mrs. Goudy said, with a little sigh.

"We could help you get there," Sam said.

"No, I'd just slow you down. You girls go ahead, but make sure you report back as soon as you find something. I haven't had this much excitement in a long time."

"We will," Sam promised, sticking the trowel and notebook into her backpack.

J.J. put away her pen. "We'll get your trowel back to you too."

"No hurry," Mrs. Goudy laughed. "I don't have any plants to repot these days."

Sam and J.J. headed straight west from the edge of the Pioneer Village parking lot. They crossed the Government House visitors parking area in as straight a line as they could, over the sidewalk and onto the grassy grounds.

Once in a while, they dodged trees or bushes or a flower bed, but they always checked back to make sure they were still in alignment with their starting point. It helped that there was a white car parked right there, and they could see it easily through the fall-coloured foliage surrounding them.

Near the west edge of the property, Sam stopped. "We better make sure no one can see us." She peered in every direction.

Traffic zoomed by on the street, but they seemed to be alone on the grounds. The sun slanted across the lawns, etching the trees and bushes in the long shadows.

"No one seems to be at the Government House any more, either," J.J. said.

"So far, so good. How about I stand here until you find the foundation piece, and then we can mark the likely corner of the staff building?" Sam said.

J.J. walked south, scanning the ground.

"Found it," she called over to Sam after a few minutes.

Sam pulled out Mrs. Goudy's diagram and studied it. She dropped her backpack on the ground where both sight lines intersected.

"Now, let's find those trees with the weird arms," Sam said.

They walked through the grounds on an angle towards Dewdney Avenue, checking each of the large elm trees.

"There's one." J.J. ran over to the first one.

Sam watched her friend touch the tree. The bent branch did look like an arm pointing to the side, as if reaching out for someone or something. She whirled around and scanned the area nearby.

Within seconds, she called, "There's the other one." She walked over to it, and then turned to face the east. "And there's the large rose garden. You stay where you are until I find the middle of it."

Sam lined up with where she thought the centre was. "Tell me when it looks like I'm halfway between the two trees," she called to J.J.

Sam walked straight west for several moments.

"About there," J.J. said.

"You stay, and I'll count the steps back to the tree." Sam walked on an angle towards J.J. When she had gone thirty steps, she dropped her backpack.

Sam walked straight back. "If we've figured this out right, then this is the centre of the small rose garden, and where you are standing should be where the bench was."

Sam joined J.J. "Not exact, but let's pretend we're sitting on a bench looking through the two trees, towards the entrance gate posts."

"What do you think about here?" J.J. asked, shuffling over a little.

"The view is a little more centered between the gate posts over this way, I think," Sam said, shuffling another foot to the north.

When she was satisfied that the location matched the diagram and notes as closely as Mrs. Goudy had given them, Sam pulled the trowel from her backpack. She and J.J. checked to see if anyone was nearby, but all was quiet, and they were alone.

"Okay, we'll go with this, then." Sam dropped to her knees.

She dug the trowel into the hard ground, trying to cut segments of rooted grass, so she could set them back over the hole later. J.J. helped her pull up the section once she loosened it.

As J.J. kept watch for intruders, Sam scraped the packed soil, scuffing up tufts of grass and bits of roots. As she got a little deeper, the dirt became powdery with little stones and came out easier.

"I think we'll have to make the hole wider," J.J. said.

"I wonder how big." Sam sat back on her heels and

surveyed her progress. "We don't even know what Lily might have buried the watch in."

"Probably something not too big, but made out of tin. Wood would rot." J.J. bent back down beside Sam.

"True," Sam said. She gritted her teeth and scratched harder around the edges. When her arm got tired, she switched hands. Gradually, she made a larger hole, but she hadn't found anything yet.

"Hot work," she said, wiping the sweat off her face and flapping her hoodie to cool down.

"Do you want me to work at it for a while?" J.J. moved close beside her.

Sam sat back on her heels and handed the trowel to J.J. "The thing is," she said, "We don't even know if we have the right spot."

"We have nothing else to go on. Besides, I don't think we're down quite deep enough to give up yet." J.J. gouged at the hole, plunging deeper with each quick scoop, flinging dirt and little stones into a pile beside her. After a frantic few minutes, she paused.

"Maybe this *isn't* the right place," she said. "In fact, we don't even know if she buried it anywhere near here. Or maybe someone else already found it and Lily doesn't know."

Sam gave her a perturbed look. "It makes sense to be around here. We must be close."

J.J. glanced at the darkening landscape. "We're almost out of light. Let's just do a little more. If we can't find it tonight, we can come back and try another place tomorrow."

Sam reached for the trowel. Blowing out a loud breath, she started scraping again, making the hole deeper and wider. She worked in a steady rhythm. Then she heard a clunk.

"This might be it." She pushed the trowel around the edge of something hard. She scraped at it. "Darn. It's only a big old rock."

"Let's stop now. We need to get home for supper." J.J. began pushing the dirt back into the hole.

Together they filled it back up and lay the grass segments over the top, tamping it down with their feet. Sam scuffed the trowel clean on the grass and tucked it into her backpack. She swung her backpack over her shoulder, and they sauntered towards the gate at Dewdney Avenue, bumping against each other's shoulders.

Sam said, "It's too bad that in later years Lily and Alice didn't confide more."

Within a split second, they were back in the past, glimpsing a moonlit sky beside a caragana hedge.

Sam looked at J.J. in horror.

CHAPTER TWELVE

"SAM, YOU BONEHEAD! Now look what you've done," J.J. wailed.

"I'm sooo sorry." Sam stared at J.J.'s stricken face, partially in shadows created by the light of the moon. "I don't know how I let myself say their names." She slapped her hand against her forehead. "Wait a minute. How did that happen when they weren't here with us?"

"Nothing makes sense any more," J.J. moaned.

Sam started pacing back and forth about four steps across the damp lawn. "Maybe it's because we are spending so much time with them. And this is where they once lived."

All at once, Sam heard J.J. laughing.

"What's so funny?" Sam whirled around to glare at her.

"Look where we are." J.J. stood at the edge of the caragana hedge.

Sam scampered over and stopped short. "The small rose garden!" She couldn't believe her eyes.

"Nice coincidence, isn't it," J.J. said, chuckling.

Although it was night time, they were looking at the rose garden from the photo with Lily and Bert in it. The bench, the trellis, all of it was the same. Except that the trailing roses weren't yet full grown.

"There's something else too," J.J. said. "We don't have to panic about getting back home. We know we just have to say their names again, and we'll return."

"Yeah, I just realized that too." Sam said with a grin. "So shall we go?"

"Wait," J.J. said, grabbing Sam's arm. "Maybe we can find the watch here." She headed for the bench and scoured the ground. "Doesn't look like the ground has been disturbed."

Sam appeared at her side, unzipped her backpack and took out the trowel. She poked around a little, but it was obvious nothing had been buried there yet.

J.J. frowned. "At least we'll have a better idea of where the rose garden was when we get back. Let's sit for a few minutes to see how the bench lines up with the gate posts."

They strolled over to the bench and sat down. Although the grounds were shrouded in darkness made deeper by the shadows from the many trees and hedges, the air was still, and the night was inviting and warm.

"I can see why Lily and Bert sat here so often," J.J. said, staring at the night sky. "The moon and all the stars would have been so beautiful when there weren't any city lights to hide them."

"One day I'm sure you'll get a camera that will take the photos you want of the stars," Sam said, settling against the back of the bench. "I can see why you want to capture the night sky."

J.J. sighed. "I suppose we should get back."

Sam leapt up. "Wait a minute. Before we go, there's

one more thing we need to do."

"Now what?" J.J. moaned.

"We can take some exact measurements!" Sam dropped her backpack beside the bench and dug out her notebook and a pen.

"I guess so," J.J. said reluctantly, "Though it's a little hard to see in the dark."

"It won't be so bad. See over there." Sam pointed. "The trees with the right-angled branches might be much smaller, but they aren't hard to spot." She hoped she'd convinced J.J. "We'll just pace out the left one, because we already know the other one is thirty steps."

"Fine. The sooner we get this done, the sooner we get to go home," J.J. mumbled.

"You measure to that tree, and I'll sketch what's behind both trees to match the angles that line up with the bench. That way, we'll have the position of the bench right when we get back home. We'll meet at the bench." Sam headed off without a backward glance.

Once this was accomplished, and the numbers written in Sam's notebook, she paced the length of the bench, while J.J. walked through the middle of the rose garden to figure out how far across it was. Then they examined the area around the bench, where the trellis posts were, and how much space there was between the bench and the trellis and the bench and the rose garden. Where they couldn't measure with their feet, they used the narrow edge of the notebook, marking down each calculation.

"That about does it, except we should measure how far the southeast corner of the building is from the bench," Sam suggested.

"That makes sense. We know for sure where that is

and where the trees are, because they're visible in our time too."

"You got it," Sam said. "We'll each take a side of the bench. Meet you at the corner." She raced off to one side of the bench, lined herself up to the corner of the building and counted silently as she walked.

Out of the corner of her eye, she could see J.J. approaching. Sam sped up just a little. So did J.J. Keeping her mind focused so she wouldn't lose count, Sam increased her rate a tad more. J.J. matched her pace for pace. Still counting, Sam speed-walked the final distance.

"108," she yelled, reaching out to touch the corner of the building first.

"Nooo!" Sam heard J.J. shriek, just as the air sizzled and she plunged to the ground.

The building had disappeared, and so had J.J.

Sam was back in present time. Without her friend.

"J.J.," screeched Sam, jumping up. She dropped the notebook and pen on the ground.

A giant lump swelled in her throat. J.J. couldn't get back by touching the corner of the building without her. She had to get back to J.J. and bring her home. But how?

Sam leapt onto the piece of foundation. She jumped up and down on it. But she stayed right where she was.

"Lily and Alice," she shouted. But nothing happened. "Alice and Lily," she yelled their names in a different order. No different. Why couldn't she get back to J.J.? Maybe they both had to touch the corner at the same time to shift backwards from the present time, but that didn't seem possible.

"J.J.," she screamed again. No answer. Sam covered her face with her hands. What was she going to do? She couldn't leave J.J. stuck in the past.

Should she run for help? But where? And who would ever believe her? Even if they did, no one would be able to figure out how to find J.J.

A huge knot twisted in Sam's stomach. She took in giant gulps of air. She mustn't panic. There had to be a way to get J.J. back.

J.J. FROZE AS Sam disappeared.

Then she rushed to the corner of the staff building, and pounded her hands against it. Up and down, and on either side, everywhere she could reach she struck it. She tried a gentle touch, she tried caressing it, she tried a quick push, but no matter how she connected to the building, she remained where she was.

All alone in the dark of night.

In the past.

"Sam," she shrieked. "Don't leave me behind. Sam, come back." She cried and screamed, but it made no difference. She was cut off from the present world.

Her knees buckled and she sagged against the building. Now what was she going to do?

"Sam," she called again. "Lily, Alice, Alice, Lily, Sam," she repeated over and over again as she touched the corner of the building. But she remained in the past.

All at once, J.J. heard scraping followed by a screech. Her heart lodged in her throat.

Suddenly, she realized someone had raised a window above her.

A head popped out, and a female voice yelled, "What's

going on out there?"

J.J. flattened herself against the wall and held her breath. She didn't dare move, but hoped she was hidden well enough in the shadows. Her heart boomed like a drum in her chest.

"Is anyone there?" the voice yelled again. Then there was murmuring, and someone mentioned something about probably some animals caterwauling.

Her heart still pounding, J.J took slow, shallow breaths and stayed tight against the wall. It seemed like an hour had passed before she heard the window screech closed again.

She waited a few more minutes, and then eased herself around the corner of the building. She had to find a way back before anyone in the past found her. They'd never believe her story, and who knows where they'd send her. She'd never get home again.

She hesitated a while longer, and then dashed over to the closest caragana hedge. Partway there, she noticed something lying beside the bench. *Sam's backpack.* Clutching it to her body like a life raft, she stumbled with it and hid herself in the lower branches of the nearby hedge.

She hoped no one would come out looking for her. Except for Sam. What was her dear friend doing right now? Was she trying to get back to J.J. in the past? But how could she? She thought they needed to be together to go back and forth in time.

J.J. wracked her brain, trying to understand how Sam had wound up going back alone.

Touching the corner of the building and calling Lily and Alice's names hadn't worked. She was all alone in the middle of the grounds, in the middle of the night. What if she never saw her family and friends again? She curled into a ball, shaking. A sob escaped from her throat.

J.J. felt completely helpless and alone.

SAM WALKED UP and down, along the piece of foundation where the side of the building had been.

She had to get J.J. back. She had to bring her home. But how? She ran the instances through her mind. They'd always had to do things together. The only exception seemed to be that Sam had to be the one to touch the corner of the building to get back from the past. They'd always said the names together too.

No, they hadn't. Either one could say George Watt.

Was that the answer? J.J. just had to say his name and go back into his time, and then say it again to get back to the present. Would J.J. figure it out? How could Sam prompt her? She sat cross-legged on the ground, closed her eyes and willed J.J. to call "George Watt."

J.J. LAY UNDER the caragana bush, swiping the tears off her face. Although the 1940s were more modern than George Watt's time, she couldn't imagine what she'd do if she was stuck in it. And she certainly couldn't just stay under the bush. She had to do *something*.

She pondered all the times she and Sam had shifted back in time together. Obviously, they had to say Lily and Alice's names together, and Sam had to be the one to touch the building, with J.J. in contact with her. What else was there?

Suddenly, a thought entered her mind, almost as if someone had said it to her: "George Watt." That was it. Either one of them could say the gardener's name and not be touching one another.

J.J. scrabbled to her feet.

If she said his name, she'd go back to his time. And if she said it again, she should be back in the present. She almost whooped with delight.

She told herself to stay calm as she swung Sam's backpack onto her shoulder. Crossing her fingers, she hoped the plan would work. She closed her eyes took a deep breath, and in a strong voice called out, "George Watt." She felt light-headed, and then a whirling sensation.

Thud!

Sam's eyes flew open as something landed a few feet in front of her.

"J.J.!" she screamed, jumping to her feet.

"Sam!" J.J. raced towards Sam.

They hugged each other for several long moments, laughing and crying.

"I thought you were gone forever," Sam said, blubbering and wiping her face with her hand.

"I thought I was too," J.J. said. "I've never been so scared in my life."

"How did you get back?" Sam asked. "I kept sending you messages, hoping you could somehow hear them."

"I think I did," she said. "At least, I did what came into

my mind." She smirked. "By the way, *you know who* says hi."

"He didn't!" Sam was flabbergasted.

J.J. nodded her head and then started laughing. "No, I never saw him. I didn't take the time to stick around. Just made sure I was in his time, and got out again."

"I'm so glad you did. And that you're back safe." Sam gave J.J. another quick hug.

"So let's go home," J.J. said. "I never want to leave it again."

"I'm sure you don't. You must have been terrified."

"Wait until I tell you how I almost got caught," J.J. said.

Sam linked her arm with J.J.'s, and they strode across the grounds, chattering.

CHAPTER THIRTEEN

THE NEXT AFTERNOON, they headed back to the edge of the Government House grounds.

"This is absolutely the last time we are searching for this watch," J.J. declared.

"I'm in complete agreement," Sam said. "If it doesn't turn up, we have no other clues to go on."

J.J. stopped walking and turned to Sam. "Just as long as we're clear."

Sam nodded. "I hope we do find it, because I don't want to keep being haunted by Lily and *you know who*."

"Maybe if we stop searching, they'll stop bugging us," J.J. suggested.

Sam shrugged. "Let's see what happens today." She swung her backpack down at the dig site and pulled out her trowel and handed her notebook to J.J.

J.J. opened the notebook and consulted their latest calculations. "I'll do the measurements from the trees to the bench. You can do the ones in a straight line from the building to the bench."

"Okay," Sam said, rolling her eyes. J.J. could be so bossy sometimes. But that was okay; at least she was in their own time, safe. Sam set down the trowel and started walking toward the foundation of the old staff building. She called to J.J. "I know so much happened at once, but do you remember how many steps you had counted when I yelled out?"

"108," she answered, without a moment of hesitation. "I was too upset to finish, but I was almost at the corner, *and*, I had a lot of time to think about it."

Sam raced to the foundation piece and counted out the steps, aiming for where she thought the bench had been. She marked the spot with the trowel. She counted out the number of steps to the other side of the bench. A few minutes later, J.J. had confirmed both measurements from the trees in order to note the angles on either side of where the bench had been.

Sam laughed when she and J.J. met up almost at the same place where they'd been digging the day before. "We were only out about a foot and a half."

"Not bad," J.J. said. She picked up the trowel Sam had left on the ground.

Within minutes, they had the top layer of lawn carved out and set aside. They took turns digging, not speaking at all as they worked.

"Probably not much deeper now," Sam said after a time. She took the trowel from J.J. and grubbed out more soil.

Clink!

Sam felt a jolt of excitement. "Hope it's not just another stone."

J.J. bent over to look. "Keep going. I think I see something metal."

As Sam gouged around the edge of the hard shape, her pulse quickened.

"It's a tin box," she said at last. "But it's stuck."

While Sam scraped and pried, J.J. pulled and wiggled on the tin. At last, they had it loose. Together, they lifted it from the hole. Sitting cross-legged on the ground, they stared at the small round cookie tin that lay between them, coated in a fine layer of dirt. The scratched lid had an old picture of the former King and Queen of England.

"So you think the watch is in it?" J.J. clasped her hands together.

Sam stared at the tin for a long minute. "Maybe." She was almost afraid to find out.

Sam wiped the dirt off the lid and clawed at it with her fingernails. But it was stuck. She and J.J. wrestled with it for a few minutes, passing it back and forth, inching the lid up little by little around its edges. Finally, the lid popped open.

Inside, there was a soft, tan leather bag that looked new. J.J. drew it out of the box and loosened the drawstring on the bag.

Hardly daring to breath, Sam held out her hands. J.J. tipped the bag, and the watch slid out.

"Oh," J.J. said. "It's gorgeous." "And still polished, just like new," Sam said. She admired the intricate carving, and then handed it to J.J.

J.J. clicked a little button, and the cover sprang open.

Sam said, "No wonder, it was so special to Geor..." She felt an elbow jab her side.

"Don't say it!" J.J. yelled.

Sam clamped a hand over her own mouth.

"I'm so glad we found it at last." J.J. held it up to see it better in the light.

"*You know who* would be so pleased to see it again,"

Sam said.

"For sure, he would. You don't suppose...nah, never mind." J.J. looked away.

Sam grinned. "I bet you were going to suggest we take it back to him."

J.J. nodded. "But I made you promise we'd never go back in time again."

"We could maybe make this one tiny exception," Sam said. "That is, if you agreed."

J.J. nodded. "We know it wouldn't take long."

"If you're up for it, I am." Sam stared hard and long at J.J.

"Okay."

They took special care to replace the watch in the leather bag and tuck it into the box. J.J. held it.

"Say it together?" Sam asked.

J.J. took Sam's hand. "One, two, three."

"George Watt."

Sam looked around. They were still in the present. "Try it again," she said.

"George Watt," they said again.

Nothing happened.

"It's not working," Sam said. "You try it by yourself."

"George Watt," J.J. said.

Still nothing.

Sam tried next.

J.J. placed the tin gently back onto the lawn. "What about now that we're not holding it?"

First, Sam tried alone, then J.J., and then they tried again together.

"Do you suppose we can't get back in time now because the watch is found?" J.J. asked.

"I bet you're right." She sighed.

"Besides, if we did take it back, what would that do with the things that happened over time? If the watch was returned, then Lily wouldn't have found it and given it to Bert."

"Sounds too messed up. It might be really dangerous to meddle with the past," Sam said. "But I wonder why we were supposed to the find the watch, then?"

"Well, if nothing else, I'm sure George would be pleased that others will be able to see his treasure," J.J. said.

Sam shook her head. "That doesn't seem like good enough reason for us to be led to search for it."

J.J. THOUGHT FOR a minute. "I agree. Especially when Mrs. Goudy and Lily got involved."

Suddenly, Lily was standing in front of them. She had a look of joy on her face.

"Thank you," she mouthed.

J.J. nudged Sam, who was staring at the tin on the ground. "Lily's here," she whispered.

J.J. and Sam stood open-mouthed as Lily walked away, and a young man joined her. Arm in arm, they strolled across the grounds. J.J. and Sam watched until they disappeared into the shadows.

J.J. felt her throat tighten. She heard a sniffle beside her. She glanced at Sam wiping at her eyes.

Suddenly, J.J. punched a fist into her other palm, startling Sam. "I know why now," she said. "Remember when we were in the basement with the class, starting our posters?"

Sam nodded.

"And we went for a drink at the fountain, and *you* wanted to explore...just before we met George?"

"Sure." Sam said.

"Before I followed you, a woman passed me as she went towards the stairs. She smiled at me. Guess what she wore?"

"Not a blue flowered dress?"

J.J. nodded vigorously. "I'm sure that was Lily."

Sam shivered. "Wow. That makes sense."

"I don't think us searching for the watch ever had anything to do with George Watt. It was Lily who wanted us to find it all along."

They stared at one another.

Sam started laughing. "Guess we solved another ghost problem."

"Let's hope it's the last one," J.J. said with a stern look. Then she broke into a smile. "At least we were able to do it together, and neither one of us are lost in the past."

"Let's hope we never are," Sam said.

They filled the dirt back into the hole and packed the lawn pieces back on top.

When they were done, J.J. said, "Let's go home. We can fill Mrs. Goudy in tomorrow."

"She'll be really excited to see the watch," Sam said. "She may decide to keep it."

"Somehow, I doubt that," J.J. said, linking arms with Sam. "She already said she'd like to donate it to the museum, so others can see it."

They hurried across the Government House grounds in the end of the day's fading light.

Once, Sam almost stopped. "I think I hear soft laughter in the shadows over there."

Shaking her head sternly, J.J. tugged Sam's arm. Without a word or a backward glance, they continued towards home.

ACKNOWLEDGEMENTS

Thank you to my incredibly diligent, meticulous, and enlightened Editor, Anne Patton – the best Editor ever. It's been a true pleasure to work with and learn from you. I hope we can do it again sometime!

Thanks to the wonderful folks at Coteau Books, for taking a chance on me once again, and for the great production and marketing team. John Agnew, MacKenzie Hamon and Susan Buck, you rock!

I'm so very grateful for the invaluable assistance, kindness and support of my research and book from the marvellous staff folks at the Government House Museum: Carrie Ross, Chad Delbert, Amanda Girardin, Sylvie Roy and Dick Stark, and the rest of the commissionaires and interpretive host staff. They tirelessly answered my questions and opened their archives to me.

Thanks, Thuraya Brennan, for reading my drafts and responding with insightful comments. You are a gem.

I am honoured to be a member of the Word Weavers writing group and can't thank each of these special friends enough for their valuable feedback and suggestions: Patricia Miller-Schroeder, Alison Lohans, Sharon Hamilton and Anne Patton.

Thanks also to my son, Aaron, and his partner Sarah; my mom, Elaine Iles; and my sister, Darlene, and her three daughters, Tayla, Zara, and Shania, for their loving support always.

I appreciate all of you more than I can express.

ABOUT THE AUTHOR

Judith Silverthorne is the multiple-award-winning Canadian author of more than a dozen books. *Convictions*, her first Young Adult historical novel, won gold in the 2016 Moonbeam Children's Writing Award for Young Adult – Historical/Cultural. She has many children's novels published, one of which has been translated into Japanese, plus two adult non-fiction biographies. Her first picture book, *Honouring the Buffalo*, published in English and Cree in 2015, is an international award winner, and in 2016 it was published in French and Cree.

The love of nature, people and history inspire Judith Silverthorne's writing and help shape many of her books. Saskatchewan-based, she travels the world acquiring knowledge of cultures and societies, exploring mysteries, experiencing significant events, and the everyday lives of people, which she weaves into her numerous stories.

Judith teaches writing classes, has presented hundreds of readings and writing workshops at libraries, schools and other educational institutions, and has given numerous presentations at conferences and literary festivals.

For more information about Judith, visit her website: www.judithsilverthorne.ca